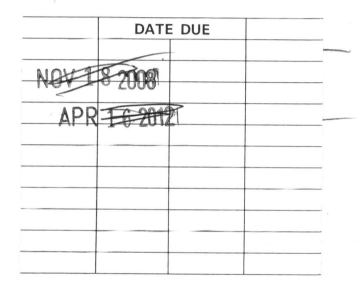

	DATE DUE		
	NOV 18 2008		
	APR 16 2012		

PHANTOMS
IN THE NIGHT

Other Five Star Titles
by Les Savage, Jr.:

Fire Dance at Spider Rock
Medicine Wheel
Coffin Gap

PHANTOMS
IN THE NIGHT

A Western Story

Les Savage, Jr.

Five Star
Unity, Maine

Five Star Western
Published in conjunction with Golden West Literary
Agency.

November 1998

First Edition, Second Printing.

Five Star Standard Print Western Series.

The text of this edition is unabridged.

Set in 11 pt. Plantin by Minnie B. Raven.

Printed in the United States on permanent paper.

Library of Congress Cataloging in Publication Data

Savage, Les.
    Phantoms in the night : a Western story /
by Les Savage, Jr. — 1st ed.
        p.   cm.
    "A Five Star western" — T.p. verso.
    ISBN 0-7862-1161-X (hc : alk. paper)
    I. Title.
PS3569.A826P47   1998
    813'.54—dc21   98-29042

PHANTOMS IN THE NIGHT

Chapter One

The wind had fallen dead, and the brig was rolling heavily. They had doused all lights, even the binnacle, and it was black as pitch on deck. John Hayward stood beside Captain Lansing at the rail, looking ashore at Monterey's lights hung against the night's satiny blackness like a strand of glowing pearls.

"Remember that Callahan is the only man in town you're to contact," Lansing said. "There isn't another soul we can trust. After you see him, you're completely on your own."

"Like a bird out of the cage," Hayward said.

Captain Lansing glanced sharply at him. "I wish you'd take it more seriously, Hayward. I've had the feeling ever since you shipped aboard that you weren't quite the man for the job."

Hayward grimaced into the night. "Beggars can't be choosers, Captain. I was the only man they could get."

Lansing snorted irritably. The creak of the winches ceased, and Hayward knew the gig had reached the water. Lansing fumbled for his hand in the darkness.

"Right man or not, John Hayward, I wish you luck. We'll be back the first of June. If they won't let us in the harbor, we'll lie off Santa Cruz. If you can't reach us personally, try to get somebody through."

Hayward flipped his head, then turned to climb down the Jacob's ladder into the gig. The bosun shoved off, and the four oarsmen bent to their task. It took them half an hour to reach the white California beach, riding in on the curling surf of low tide. As soon as they grounded, Hayward jumped out, and two others followed him, swinging the boat around. The bosun turned toward him, speaking huskily.

"I knew you wasn't a sailor the minute you shipped aboard, Hayward. I never guessed this was what they brought you for."

"You'll read about it in the Boston papers," Hayward said, grinning. "Better cast off now, Bo."

He knew a moment of keen loneliness as he watched them pull out through the surf. Then he shook his head and turned to walk down the beach. Monterey in 1845 was not much of a town. Most of its tile-roofed buildings were bunched around the plaza and along the Calle Principal, which was the main street. Its night life centered around the saloons near the water front. One of these was the Pacific Building, a seaman's tavern built in 1835 by Harry Callahan, one of the first Americans in Monterey. Light from its slot-like windows spilled yellow stripes across the muddy street. In this treacherous dappling of light and shadow, the white cotton shirts of passing townsmen blossomed out of the darkness like great moths whenever they crossed a band of light.

As Hayward approached the building, he heard the clatter of a coach coming from the upper end of the street. At the same time, a man appeared in a band of light streaming from the first window of the Pacific Building. He was a short man, broad as a bear, rolling from side to side on his bowed legs and singing a drunken song.

**Ojos trigueños, color de café,
Dame un beso de buena fé. . . .**

The rattle of wheels and jingle of harness drowned his

8

song as the coach came racing down the street. His head bent, his bleary eyes half closed, he seemed oblivious of it. Hayward shouted a warning, but the sound of the coach blotted out his voice. In another moment it would run the man down. Hayward lunged at the man, knocking him aside and against the wall. The driver of the coach was standing on the footboards and sawing on the reins to veer the horses and pull them to a halt. He almost smashed into the building across the street before he brought the coach to a stop.

"You pig!" he shouted. "Out of the way!"

The thickset man recovered himself, glanced at Hayward, then turned toward the coach. He spread his legs and settled his massive shoulders belligerently. "Who calls Miguel Corado a pig?"

A woman leaned from the window of the coach. Hayward had a vivid impression of her, in that moment, revealed by light from the building. A Spanish comb in blue-black hair, half hidden by the lace of a white mantilla, eyes that flashed like jewels in the pale cameo of a face. The snowy upper slopes of melon-ripe breasts swelled from a tightly laced bodice.

"Corado," she said. "Can't you see who it is?"

"Of course, I see," Corado replied. "It is one of the *ricos* who ride about in their coaches and run down the *peones* as if they were pigs in the mud."

"Corado!" It came sharply, from the woman in the coach. "Come here."

The man swayed, blinking his eyes. Hayward saw that he wore the rawhide jacket and pants and the flat-heeled wing boots of a cattleman from the interior. Finally he walked to the coach. When he reached the door, he stopped. The woman spoke again.

9

"Now, do you still wish to insult me?"

Hayward saw recognition enter the man's bleary eyes. For a moment, however, the anger and the sardonic mockery still remained in his coarse-featured face. But the woman's eyes bored into his, and finally a little muscle twitched in his swarthy cheek, and he swept off his yellow sombrero, bowing low.

"A thousand pardons, *Señorita* Mateo. I was drunk and truly did not know who I was talking to."

Her voice was thin with impatience. "The next time it happens, I'll have the hide flayed from your back."

She settled into the seat; the driver flicked his whip; the team broke into a trot down the main street. Corado stared after the black coach a long time. The expression on his primitive face was paradoxical. His splayed nostrils fluttered like those of an enraged horse; his thick lips were pinched tight with anger. But there was a shining glow to his eyes that held no rage at all. It was a strange moment, holding Hayward fascinated. Finally, as if released from a trance, Corado seemed to become aware of him again.

"*¿Habla español?*"

"Yes," Hayward said in Spanish, "I speak your language."

"Why did you save my life?" the man asked.

"They would have run you down."

"But you are an American."

"Does that make any difference?"

The man studied him a minute, running his eyes over his tall frame. The heavy blue seaman's coat hid the whiplash leanness of Hayward's body, the powerful breadth of his shoulders. His face held a raw, bony handsomeness, with deep-socketed eyes and a long-lipped mouth, curling with humor at the tips. He wore no hat on his corn-yellow hair, and it had grown so long during the months at sea that he had clubbed it behind his neck and tied it with a black ribbon. The other man finally broke into a rough laugh.

"Of course, it does not matter. You saved my life, and we will have a drink on it."

Hayward realized it would probably be better for him to enter the saloon in the company of a Californian than alone. "How about the Pacific House?" he asked.

"As good as any. I am Corado, the *amansador* of Rancho del Sur. And you are a sailor."

"Who was busy with a girl yesterday when the longboat put back to my brig," Hayward said. "Now I'm looking to get back on the *Noah* before she sails."

Corado moved over to him, redolent of chili and wine and sweat that had not been washed from his body in a month. "Perhaps we will find someone with a boat in the Pacific House," he said.

Arm in arm they entered the inn. Its taproom was one long chamber, smoke-blackened beams of immense size supporting the ceiling. There was a thin line of men at the bar, and half the heavy round tables in the dining section were occupied. The whole place reeked of steaming beans and sour leather and sweet wine. Hayward saw the heads begin to pop up at sight of his blond hair, and heard someone mutter.

"None of that," Corado shouted. "*Americano* or not, he is my friend, and we will drink together. Do you wish to argue about that? Do you wish to argue with Corado?"

The muttering subsided, and one by one the sullen faces dipped back to their drinks or their conversation. Corado escorted Hayward to the bar, and they ordered mescal. A ripe-breasted serving girl passed with an empty

11

tray, and Corado caught her, swinging her casually to him.

"This is Nita," he told Hayward. "She is madly in love with me. All the women in California love me."

She squealed and giggled as he pulled her plump body against him and kissed her fully on the lips. Hayward took that chance to sneak a look around for Callahan. He saw the kitchen door swing open, and a potbellied, red-headed man in greasy blue jeans and a padded marseilles waistcoat came out. He walked up the bar to Hayward, taking his arm.

"Listen, bucko, you got to get back to your brig. I thought that was made plain to your captain yesterday. The *alcalde*'s closed the port to Yankee ships, and, if they find any of you sailors in my place, we'll both be strung up by the thumbs."

Corado was too drunk and too fully occupied with Nita to notice anything else, and Hayward allowed the man to lead him toward the front. He made his grin tipsy, his voice slurred.

"I ain't trying to smuggle any hides out. I just want to line my scuppers with grog for that haul around the Horn. Have a last drink with me before I cast off."

Corado shouted over Nita's shoulder: "Let him stay, Callahan. He is my friend. I will wreck the place, if you don't."

Callahan frowned, tugging at his sparse red beard. "All right," he said. "One drink."

They were near a table in an unoccupied corner of the room, and he pulled out a chair and sat down. "You Hayward?" he asked in English.

"Isn't this a little public? Why couldn't I have come to your quarters?"

"Yankees can't move far in this town without being

12

spotted. If they saw you sneaking up my back stairs, they'd really get suspicious. Out here you're just another tar that's shipped aboard too much grog. Now we're out of earshot and not many of these people speak English, anyway. Tell me what you know, and I'll fill in the rest."

Hayward tried to look casually drunk, talking in a conversational tone. "Washington City just got news of Roger Bardine's disappearance a few months ago. As I understand it, Bardine was respected by these people."

Callahan nodded, digging a cutty pipe from his waistcoat pocket. "Roger Bardine came here in Eighteen Thirty-Six, swore fealty to the Mexican government, even married a Monterey woman. In Eighteen Forty-Four, he became the first United States consul in California. A few months later, Andrés Rodríguez was appointed *alcalde* of Monterey. It's a post that gives a man power out of proportion to the office. One of the first things *Alcalde* Rodríguez did was to close Monterey to Yankee ships. Since Monterey is the only official port of entry, all foreign vessels had to register their cargo here before disposing of it, and that virtually cut the whole of California off from any trade with the Americans. *Alcalde* Rodríguez evidently presented valid reasons for his act to the governor, because Pico hasn't interfered. You know what a big business this hide trade has become."

Hayward nodded. "The shippers claim they've lost several hundred thousand dollars already."

"Right. As consul, Bardine started objecting. There was even a rumor that he had started a move to depose *Alcalde* Rodríguez. Then, in December of last year, Bardine disappeared."

"Rodríguez did it?"

Callahan held a match to the pipe, sucked on it assiduously. "That's the local conclusion. But all we know for

13

sure is that Bardine's daughter told us half a dozen men came and took Bardine away by force one night. That's why we think he's still alive somewhere. If they wanted to kill him, they'd have done it on the spot. Drink some of that . . . make this look real."

Another serving girl had brought mescal in a clay jug. Hayward poured it and took a gulp, squinting his eyes against its raw fire. "Washington City has the idea that Bardine's disappearance is only a part of what's happening."

Callahan nodded. "A small part. But I think he's the key to it. Somebody's deliberately whipping up feeling against the Yankees. Even the old-timers like me aren't safe on the streets now."

"*Alcalde* Rodríguez again?"

"That would be a logical conclusion," Callahan said, "but it's a treacherous one. There are too many other things involved. You get into local politics, now. California has always been a place for intrigue. There are always half a dozen different factions seeking power. Any one of the groups could be back of this new trouble. It's too complicated to explain in a minute. You'll have to unravel that part as you go along."

"Any idea where they've taken Bardine?"

"Inland somewhere. They couldn't stay close to town without word leaking through." Callahan pursed his lips, studying Hayward. "So how's the Spanish?"

"*Soy un tipo modesto, como ya ve, pero debo dármelas de experto. Puedo hablar hasta por los codos. Por si acaso no me cree. . . .*"

Callahan held up a hand to stop Hayward, grinning wryly. "All right, all right. I should be kicked for asking that, but you look so damn' Yankee."

"I was born in Mexico City," Hayward said. "My fa-

14

ther was a military *attaché* there."

"So you're all Army."

Hayward nodded. "West Point and everything. Same class as Captain Frémont, incidentally. I understand he's been seen here."

"He has," Callahan scowled. "Supposed to be traveling through California with some topography expedition. I don't think he's fooling anybody. Is he hunting Bardine, too?"

"Nobody knows what his official orders are," Hayward said. "But if Frémont's hunting Bardine, he must have failed, because he's the one who recommended me for this job." Hayward stopped, studying Callahan, who was frowning at the table and drumming his fingers on its splintery top. Hayward leaned toward him. "I have the feeling there's something you haven't told me."

Callahan's pipe had gone out, and he knocked it irritably against the table. He seemed reluctant to speak. "Did Lansing mention *los fantasmas en la noche?*"

"The phantoms in the night?" Hayward chuckled. "Sounds melodramatic."

Callahan knocked his pipe against the table again, scowling at Hayward. "I can't quite see why Frémont would recommend a man like you. You're treating this whole thing as a joke."

Hayward leaned toward him. "Listen, Callahan, this is just a job to me." He was grinning, but he was irked. "Just a trip on a boat and a stopover at a place that doesn't look any different than a hundred other places I've seen."

"Hayward, I didn't. . . ."

"I spent most of Eighteen Forty-Two in the Santa Fé pestholes Arleta called his dungeons to get those Texas freebooters out. I got smallpox begging in the streets of Tripoli to find out if they were going to declare another war on us,

15

got malaria down in Sinaloa trying to discover if Lafitte was really still alive, dysentery in Cuba breaking up the Povero revolt, six inches of steel in my liver making sure another French and Indian war didn't start in Ottawa. Now just how much of a tragedy do you want me to make out of this?"

"Take it easy." Callahan held up a hand, looking surprised. "I didn't mean to get so personal."

Hayward settled back. "Forget it. I guess too many people have been climbing down my craw this evening. Captain Lansing was riding me about the same thing. I'm sorry I can't regard every job as if it was my own funeral, but it's just an old story to me, and I'm naturally a happy guy, anyway, and that's the way I do things. You wouldn't want a surgeon to get sentimental about an operation. He'd botch it."

Callahan put his pipe back in his mouth, laughing huskily. "Grin, then, you jackanapes."

"I am," Hayward said. "Now, what about these phantoms in the night?"

"That will have to wait. I see Ugardes coming this way. He's the *alcalde*'s right-hand man."

Ugardes wound through the tables like a snake. He had a pale face for such a sunny country, a pale wedge of a face with great waxen hollows beneath his gaunt cheekbones and eyes like black beads. He was dressed in tightly fitting trousers of rusty red buckskin, slit traditionally to the knee to reveal the immaculate linen beneath, with a red sash wound a dozen times around his narrow waist, and a gold-frogged jacket tailored impeccably to his narrow shoulders. He stopped in front of Hayward, moistening his lips before he spoke.

"*¿Habla español?*"

"*Sí,*" Hayward said.

The man assayed a formal bow, speaking in his native tongue. "*Alcalde* Rodríguez requests your presence."

Hayward caught a negative movement of Callahan's head, a warning flash of his eyes, and took his cue. He played the drunk again, speaking loosely. "The *alcalde* wants to see me . . . tell him to come here."

"*Señor,*" Ugardes said impatiently, "you are breaking the law by being ashore. If you do not come at once, troops will be sent after you, and you will go to jail."

Corado had pushed Nita aside to watch, and he shouted across the room to Ugardes. "Why did Rodríguez not send dragoons in the first place, Ugardes? Is this another one of his underhanded schemes?"

"You stay out of this," Ugardes told him. His eyes glittered at Hayward. "Are you coming?"

"Don't do it," Corado called. "They're up to something. If it were official, the dragoons would have come."

As Hayward remained in his seat, impatience made a ridge of whitened flesh about Ugardes's compressed lips. He turned aside, speaking to three men at a wall table. "The American is causing trouble, Luis. Will you and your friends help me escort him to the *alcalde?*"

The men scraped back their chairs and rose and came to surround Hayward. When they saw he still did not mean to rise, two of them grabbed his arms and jerked him on his feet. He let them get that far and then sank his elbow viciously into the belly of the man on his right and kicked the other man hard in the knee. They both fell away with pain in their faces, and he wheeled to run. But the third man caught his arm, trying to pull him back. At the same time, Corado staggered through the tables from the bar and grabbed that man, tearing him off Hayward and sending him spinning.

17

"Leave him alone!" he shouted. "He saved my life."

But he could hardly be heard over the uproar of shouts and toppling chairs. Half the men in the room were already on their feet, and the others were throwing their chairs back and jumping up. The expressions on their faces made Hayward realize for the first time how bad the feeling was against Americans. Their eyes held something avid, like those of animals eagerly anticipating a kill. The rush of their feet made the floor tremble, and their yelling deafened Hayward. Callahan tried to jump up, but his chair was torn from beneath him, and he fell into the rush of men and disappeared. Hayward wheeled to meet the first man, who came from his flank, dodging his clumsily swung fist and clouting him across the face. As he fell back, Hayward saw Ugardes circling the table with a knife.

Hayward wheeled back, but the man was already in close, thrusting low. All Hayward could do was kick at the blade. His heavy shoe struck Ugardes's hand with a sharp crack. The man's face contorted with pain, and he staggered back, grabbing his hand. Another man charged into Hayward's shoulder, knocking him against the table. Hayward hit him full in the face and saw him fall aside with a bloody nose. Corado had leaped atop the table, kicking away a man who sought to pull him down.

"It's going to be a fight for good, *amigo*," he bawled. "Get up here, and we'll meet them back to back."

Hayward sat on the table, kicking into the belly of a man who rushed him. The man doubled over, and Hayward had time to gain his feet on the table. Corado scooped up the jug of mescal and smashed it across the head of a man who swiped at him with a knife. Another tried to upset the table, and Corado wheeled to kick him.

Hayward pivoted around till his back was against the

18

hot, sweating back of Corado. Someone swept a chair at him. He caught it in mid-air, wrenching it free, and threw it into the sea of faces. Then he swung around toward a trio of men who were trying to upset the table. Corado kicked one of them in the face. A second caught his leg, trying to spill him. Hayward stamped on the man's arm, and the man let Corado go with a howl. Corado bent down and caught the third one by his hair, lifting him bodily off the floor and heaving him back into the struggling mass behind.

"We are invincible!" Corado screamed. His swarthy face was exalted with the drunken excitement of battle.

But there were too many of them, coming from all sides. Hayward wheeled to kick one away, and another caught his leg, pulling him to one knee. A dozen hands pawed at him. He slugged blindly at faces and stamped on a fist, as he tried vainly to get back on his feet again.

"*¡Los dragones!*" somebody shouted. "The dragoons!"

Hayward saw a blue uniform appear in the doorway of the inn. With a mighty effort he tore free, kicking a face away, driving up once more to put his back against Corado's. Then a thrown bottle hit him on the side of the head. Lights flashed before him, and he felt himself pitching forward off the table. Then the lights went out.

Chapter Two

Hayward returned to a consciousness filled with the smells of mud and unwashed bodies and dank adobe. He opened his eyes to a gauzy light that came through a single barred window and fell across the vague outlines of men huddled together in a small room. He realized it was morning, and he was lying on his back in the mud, squeezed between the inert bodies of two snoring men. Wincing at the pain in his head, he looked around the room until he found Corado. The man was grinning.

"That bottle put you to sleep all night. Now that you are awake, come and stand against the wall so somebody else can sleep a while."

Hayward got unsteadily to his feet. The men on the floor were pressed so tightly together that he had to jam a foot down between two bodies every time he took a step. As soon as he left his spot, a dozen men lurched away from the walls, stumbling across the bodies in their effort to gain the empty space first. An Indian was the lucky one, dropping full length into the place. The other men cursed him roundly and went back to the wall, heedless of the grumbles and groans of pain from the men they stepped on. Hayward took his stand beside Corado, and the man clapped him on the back.

"That was a magnificent fight. Last time I had to stand alone against the whole bunch of them. It lasted twice as long with two of us, and afforded me twice as much pleasure. You like to fight, *hombre?*"

"Nothing like it in the world," Hayward said.

"Except drinking."

"Except drinking."

"And wenching."

"That above all."

Corado roared with laughter, hitting him on the back again. "You are a man after my own heart. If we were only out of this stink hole, what a time we would have! I could show you a thousand wenches, Hayward, and more mescal than the ocean could hold."

Hayward did not answer, but looked around the over-crowded room, with its stench of unwashed bodies, its bare walls, its floor of viscid mud. He knew these prisons, and how long a foreigner could stay here, forgotten. To know that he had failed his mission so miserably before he had even started was almost unbearable to him. Then he grinned, remembering Callahan, and last night. He had gone through worse. Just another job, and, if it took that long, well, what the hell?

From outside there was a murmur of voices, then a chain rattled, and the heavy oaken door was pulled open. Some of the men nearest the opening crowded into the door, speaking rapidly in Spanish. They were shoved roughly back, a couple tripping and falling into the sleeping men. Hayward saw that a corporal stood in the doorway, dressed in the round blue jacket of a dragoon, with its red cuffs and collar. Behind him was Ugardes in his rusty buckskins. There was a bandage on his right hand. His beady eyes scoured the room till they found Hayward. His voice had a silken hiss.

"Perhaps you will see the *alcalde* now."

Hayward shrugged, and moved across the bodies. The corporal told Corado that his presence was wished, also, and he followed Hayward across the packed bodies. The

21

room was filled with curses and groans as his clanking spurs ripped at hide and cloth. There was another pair of dragoons behind the corporal, and they flanked Hayward. Ugardes watched Hayward a moment, an unreadable expression on his wedge-like face. Then he turned and led the way across the sunlit plaza, past the long barracks, where more troops lounged, to a tile-roofed house of adobe bricks, completely surrounded by a high, vine-covered wall. They went through the gate, across a tree-shaded patio, into the living room. It was cool and gloomy in here, and richly furnished for such a distant frontier. The floors were earthen, but almost completely covered with luxurious Brussels carpets. The room seemed crowded with zebra-wood sideboards and mahogany tables and gleaming drum tables covered with the blinding glitter of cut-glass carafes and decanters. In all this sumptuous confusion, it took Hayward a moment to pick out *Alcalde* Rodríguez, seated at a breakfast table near one of the heavily draped windows.

He was a gross, big-bellied man, completely overflowing the fragile chair in which he sat. His black hair was showing gray at the temples, with carefully tended sideburns curling out almost to the tips of his sensual lips. His great thighs strained at blue velvet trousers. Before him were spread the remains of an enormous breakfast. As Hayward stopped a dozen feet from him, he squinted his eyes in an effort to see, then beckoned impatiently.

"Come here, come here."

Hayward moved closer, into the strong floral scent of the man's perfume.

Rodríguez toyed with a fork, squinting up at him. "So you got left behind when I sent Captain Lansing back to his boat."

22

They must have told him Hayward spoke Spanish, for he spoke in that language.

"I was busy," Hayward said.

"With one of those wenches behind the Pacific Building, I'd wager," Rodríguez said. He plucked a grape from a bunch by his breakfast plates, popped it into his mouth. "Then you got drunk last night and tried to kill Ugardes."

Hayward knew this was the time for conciliation. He couldn't afford to antagonize the man further. "I hope you'll forgive me, *señor*. I was drunk. I can't even remember what I did."

"You did enough." Rodríguez turned suddenly, jabbing the fork into Hayward's belly. "Are you a spy?"

It was not a painful jab, only a gesture to emphasize the question, but Hayward could not help jumping.

Behind him, Corado laughed roughly. "A spy? What a joke! He could not hide that yellow hair in a tar barrel. Would they pick someone fool enough to make a fight with every man in town when he is first here?"

"Hold your peace," Rodríguez told him. "You will be judged when your turn comes." He shifted his weight forward and heaved his bulk out of the chair. Then he held his arms stiffly out behind him. "Ugardes?"

The narrow man moved swiftly at Hayward's flank, taking a fancy velvet jacket from where it hung on the chair and holding it for Rodríguez. The *alcalde* shrugged into it and moved over to a huge baroque pier glass. He pouted, frowned at himself in the mirror, postured this way and that, tugging peevishly at the jacket, shaking out the lace on his cuffs.

"If you are not a spy," he said, "what are you?" He turned, pointing a fat finger at Hayward. "Mind your answer. I am a shrewd judge of men. I can see by the way

23

you stand that you have been a sailor all your life. But that does not fool me. Sailors can be spies, too."

"Why are you so afraid of spies?" Hayward asked.

"I am surrounded by spies," Rodríguez said spitefully. "The governor sends his spies. They send spies from Mexico City. The French are planning to take over California. The Russians are trying to come down from the north. I can trust no one."

"*Señor* . . . ," Ugardes protested.

"I am sorry, Ugardes." Rodríguez fluttered a conciliatory hand toward him. "I know you will stand by me till the end. In all the world I have only you." He wheeled on Hayward, pointing at him again. "Why did you not come last night? Why did you try to wreck the town?"

"I was told I'd broken a law. I was told I would be put in jail."

"I think it was natural to put up a fight," said a woman's voice from the corner. "I would have fought to keep from going to jail, particularly if I was drunk."

Hayward turned in surprise. The gloom at the far corner of the room was so deep that he had not noticed her there, sitting on a settee, half hidden behind a fancy rosewood armoire. It was the woman he had seen last night in the coach. In the dim light, the upper slopes of her breasts above the tight bodice had a seductive swell. She saw Hayward's glance stop boldly there, and a quick, proud flush ran into her cheeks. She opened her fan across her bosom, regarding him with snapping eyes over its edge.

"I did not come to hear you question a drunken sailor, *señor*," she said. "You will tell me what sentence you have passed on my *amansador*."

Rodríguez frowned at Corado, lips pouted indulgently. "Why are you such a naughty child, Corado? Am I not

24

beset with enough difficulties?" He sighed, turning to the woman. "His sentence shall be a month this time, Carlota. But I will release him with a fine of twenty *pesos* and your promise that he will be barred from town for eight weeks."

She nodded her promise, and rose with a sensuous hiss of silk. Corado moved up beside Hayward, speaking to her.

"I am your slave, *patrona*. But I have one request to make before we go. It is for the man who saved my life twice last night. You know it is often the custom for the imprisoned American sailors to work out their sentences, instead of rotting in that pigsty we call a jail. With half our riders deserting into the hills, we need whatever help we can get."

"This is foolishness," Rodríguez said. "I think the man is a spy, and, until we are sure, he is too dangerous to let out of town."

"Perhaps you are right," Corado said. "Colonel Archuleta would not favor it."

Rodríguez's gross head snapped up, and his eyes rolled like marbles in his head. "What has Archuleta got to do with it? I am in command here."

Corado pursed his thick lips. "I thought, perhaps, you feared to flout the colonel's wishes. It is said that Archuleta warned it would go badly with anyone showing the American leniency."

"Leniency? Who is showing him leniency? Six months of backbreaking labor on your ranch will make him understand our laws better than ten years of lounging around our prison. And what right has Archuleta to threaten me, anyway? It is my wish, *señorita*, that you take this man, and report on his conduct every month."

Corado grimaced. "But, *señor*, the good Colonel Archuleta will not like. . . ."

25

"The colonel has nothing to do with this," stormed Rodríguez. "I run this town. It is more than my wish, it is my order that you take. . . ." He caught himself up, turning apologetically to Carlota Mateo. "A thousand pardons. I did not mean to use such a tone with you. But, as Corado says, you do need the help. You were only asking me yesterday if I could not find some men in town for you."

Hayward thought there was a sparkle of mischief in her eyes. Her lips were hidden behind the fan. "And I will have nothing to fear from Archuleta?"

Rodríguez's face darkened, but he contained himself with better success. "Believe me, Carlota, you have *my* protection. The colonel has nothing whatsoever to say about this, and, if he so much as raises a finger in your direction. . . ."

She bowed her head demurely. "I accept your protection with great gratitude, and I will take the prisoner, if you are sure he knows his place."

Corado grinned, clapping Hayward on the back. "I will keep him in his place."

And Hayward knew he would.

Chapter Three

They brought Corado his horse and gave Hayward a mount from the ample saddle strings of the dragoons. Carlota Mateo's black coach, followed by the two riders, left the town and rose into the pine-covered hills behind Monterey and finally dropped down into the Salinas Valley beyond. They traveled for hours through wild oats and yellow mustard that grew so tall Corado often had to stand in the saddle to see ahead.

The horse they had given Hayward was a half-broken mustang with a rough trot, but Corado was magnificently mounted. He rode a black stallion with so much spirit that it fretted incessantly at the bit and pranced from side to side in a constant lather to break into a gallop. The man possessed a handsome saddle, stamped in green and gold, with a *sobrejalma* behind the cantle, a gorgeous housing made from the pelt of a Sonora tiger cat. His bridle and spurs were inlaid with beaten silver, and on the stirrups were the usual *tapaderos,* the fenders of bullhide that kept his toes from snagging in the brush. They were silver-plated and hand-carved and were so long their tips kept brushing through the wild flowers on the ground. He sat his fiddling animal with a casual seat and a tight rein, and all through the afternoon he kept chuckling to himself about Rodríguez.

"Did you see my strategy? I should be a diplomat. *Alcalde* Rodríguez hates Colonel Archuleta. The minute he finds out Archuleta wants something, he is automatically opposed to it. I think he would cut off his own arm to flout Archuleta's wishes."

Hayward realized this was probably part of the political ramifications Callahan had talked of, and prodded for more. "I understand there's always been rivalry between the military and civil officials here."

"*Verdad,*" Corado agreed. "It is *Alcalde* Rodríguez's greatest ambition to become governor of California. Being *alcalde* of Monterey has often led to that. But Archuleta disagrees violently with the policies of Rodríguez. *Alcalde* Rodríguez stands in deathly fear that Colonel Archuleta will have him deposed here before he can step into the chair of the governor."

"Is Rodríguez from Mexico?"

Corado laughed. "He claims he is a Spaniard of pure descent, but we all know what a lie that is. His family was merely a tool of the Spanish crown before Mexico broke away from Spain twenty-five years ago. He is mostly *indio* from up around Yerba Buena. You will find that true of many people in California, Juanito. Some of the finest families here started with a wild Indian back in the mountains."

"And these *fantasmas en la noche . . . ?*"

Corado turned sharply, cutting him off, the different blood of anger running into his swarthy cheeks till they looked almost black. "Where did you hear that?"

Hayward thought quickly. "That girl I stayed with the night before last spoke of it. Phantoms in the night, she said."

"She is crazy. There is no such thing, just the drooling of foolish women who use it to scare their children."

"But what is it?"

"It is nothing. I don't wish to talk of it any more."

Corado touched the black with the spurs, and it broke into a gallop after the coach. Hayward realized he had made a blunder and followed the man, speaking no more.

They were passing cattle now, grazing in the head-high mustard, their flanks bearing the intricate corona brand of Rancho del Sur. They rose through chaparral growing rank and high, forming dense thickets of thorn-like branches and leathery leaves. Then the thick strands of fir closed in about them, blotting out the sun with its bristling foliage. They were in the mountains now, and they entered a cañon where redwoods towered like giants over the gnarled white-barked sycamores. The coach sought a shelving road that led them up to a broad plateau that stretched for a mile into the sunset. And at the far end of the broad mesa, backed up against a slope black with timber, stood the buildings of Rancho del Sur.

There was a big house, with its countless rooms and adobe-walled patios sprawling over half an acre of ground. Beyond it was the jackstraw pattern of a dozen corrals, large and small, teeming with stock. On the other side of the corrals were the quarters of the peons, squalid adobe huts with thatched roofs and rawhide doors. Hayward had hoped to see Carlota Mateo again, but the coach turned up toward the big house, and Corado led on to the other quarters.

As they reached the corrals and stepped down to unsaddle and turn their horses into a pen, a whole stream of children descended upon them from the dooryards of the houses. There were babies stark naked, little girls with enormous eyes and dirty cotton dresses, barefooted boys of nine and ten with long black hair and nothing on but breechclouts.

They swarmed all over Corado, tugging at his clothes, jumping on his back. Chuckling, cursing affectionately, the man pulled a bag of sticky cactus candy from his pocket and distributed it. Then he took a pair of naked babies on his shoulders and marched pompously to one of the squalid adobe houses, surrounded by the squealing, screaming children.

An old man sat in the dirt, leaning against the wall. His paunch was a magnificent edifice erected to the delights of tortillas and wine. His face was a crumbling façade seamed by the weather and grooved by experience and wrinkled by time.

"This is El Sombrío," Corado told Hayward. "The Gloomy One."

"The crops will surely be bad this year," El Sombrío said. "I saw a black crow over my left shoulder last Sunday."

Corado grinned broadly. "Do not pay attention to him. In all his fifty years on the ranch, not one of his predictions has come true. Now come in and eat."

The children followed, shouting and giggling and swarming all over Corado. The inside was typical of these dank, low-roofed adobe houses. The floor was earth, hard as cement. The furniture consisted of a few halved logs pegged together for a table and a pair of benches. The only light came from the fire crackling in the cone-shaped oven in one corner. There were three women in the room, cooking and preparing dinner. At their first sight of Corado, two of them squealed with pleasure and ran to him. He grabbed them both and planted sloppy kisses on their willing mouths, and then swung them around for Hayward's inspection.

"This is the Gloomy One's niece, Teresa. This one is Maruca, the sister of Gregorio, who works here. That one still cooking is the Gloomy One's sixth wife, Nieves. Now sit down and make love and eat."

He shoved the one named Maruca at Hayward. Hayward was knocked backward, and he had to sit down on the bench to keep from falling. Corado had almost seated himself, and he pulled Teresa onto his knee, kissing her all over the neck and bare shoulders while she squealed and kicked and pounded him in affected indignation. Hayward took the cue and pulled Maruca to him. She came willingly, letting her plump weight drop into his lap. She was about twenty, with a primitive beauty to her succulent lips, her dancing eyes, her shining black hair.

El Sombrío's wife brought them a plate of dripping ribs. She was older than the other two and already beginning to lose some of her early beauty. But her eyes were black and lustrous, settling affectionately on Corado.

"Is he not outrageous?" she said. "I do not think there is a woman within a thousand miles he has not kissed."

"More than kissed," Corado said slyly, grabbing her by the arm and pulling her down to plant his lips on hers. He made a loud smacking sound. Nieves tore free and slapped him in the face, and then laughed indulgently and went back to the fire. Corado turned and started on the ribs. He ate like some animal, fondling Teresa and kissing her between bites, heedless of the juice that dribbled down his chin, the wine he spilled on himself and the table. Hayward ate, too, holding a rib for Maruca to nibble on.

There was a clean scent to her, and the feel of her in his arms was soft and warm and completely animal. This was the part that made some of these jobs bearable, and he hoped it would be like this all the time. When they were through with the ribs, Nieves brought another covered plate. Corado wiped grease from his lips with the back of a hairy hand, speaking with a full mouth.

"This you will like, Juanito. It's a bread pudding with layers of apples and butter and sugar and cheese browned

31

on top, dusted with cinnamon, and served with hot wine sauce. In all the world nobody can make it better than Nieves."

After they were stuffed with the pudding, there was more wine. They were all half drunk, and Corado's lovemaking was becoming even more outrageous. El Sombrío sat against the wall with a flute.

"I got this from a *penitente* in Santa Fé," he said. "I will play you a funeral march."

Hayward realized Maruca was winding her fingers in his hair. "So beautiful," she murmured. "Pure gold."

"And just for you," he said tipsily. "I'll give you a pound of it for a kiss."

She pouted, her face flushed with wine. "I want all of it."

"Then I'll take the kiss for nothing," he said, and bent her back over the table. It had been a long time on that ship without a woman, and he made up for it. She struggled at first. Then she subsided. When he finally pulled away, she still lay back on the table, eyes closed, breath swelling her breasts. The room was strangely quiet, and Hayward looked up to see Corado staring round-eyed at Maruca. The man let out a low whistle.

"*¡Caramba!*" he said. "You are a lover, too." He turned enthusiastically to El Sombrío. "Did you see that? Not only is he a fighter, he is a lover." He wheeled to Nieves. "How would you like to be kissed like that, Sixth Wife? Did you ever see such a kiss?" He whacked his thigh, throwing back his head to laugh hoarsely. "You are a man after my own heart, Juanito. A fighter and a lover. All we got left is the drinking. If you can drink like you can fight and love, you will be my *compadre*. Bring on the mescal, Nieves. I will break my old record tonight. Seventeen quarts before dawn.

32

Can you keep up, Juanito?"

"What about those horses?" El Sombrío asked. "If we ride tomorrow, you better go down and see which ones we take."

Corado settled back, frowning. Then he nodded grumpily. "You are right, Gloomy One. The drinking will have to wait, Juanito." He whacked Teresa's plump buttocks, making her jump off his knee with a sharp cry, and then rose to his feet, belching hugely. "Show my friend where to sleep, Nieves. He has been in the saddle all day, and that is much more tiring than the deck of a ship. And you better come with us, Maruca. If Gregorio finds you making love to an American, he will kill you."

Maruca gazed at Hayward with misty eyes, and they had to pull her away. As they all tramped out, Hayward turned to see Nieves still looking after Corado.

"A rare man," he said.

"A beast," she said. "A clown. A lecher. A drunk. If anybody else acted the way he does, he would be hung in the morning."

"But you love him."

She clenched her teeth. "We would die for him."

He sat there silently, watching her, as she continued to stare out the door. Finally she became aware of his gaze and dropped her head self-consciously, turning to look at him from beneath her brows.

"And you, Golden One. You are not far behind him. Even Corado would have to work to equal that kiss. If I were not married, I would like to sample it myself."

He grinned. "It could be done."

She made a face at him, shooing him out with one hand. "Get out in the fresh air. If you don't clear that wine from your head, your mouth will taste like horse droppings in the morning."

33

He followed her advice and went outside. A great sense of peace lay over the line of little houses. Their lights glowed against the satin night like great fireflies, and the syrupy smell of sun-heated pitch had not yet died in the air. From somewhere near the corrals a man was playing a guitar and nearer by a baby was chortling. Nieves came out in a few minutes, saying she had to get the wash, and disappeared in the poplar grove at the end of the lane. Hayward lounged against the wall, trying to put together what he had learned today. Rodríguez's suspicion of him could not be too great, or the man would not have let him go so easily. But that answered nothing. And who were the phantoms in the night whom Corado seemed so unwilling to discuss? It was all a jumble of pieces that did not yet fit together, and he knew the futility of conjecture.

Someone was approaching. The band of light streaming from the open door licked up bare brown legs, caught on a flickering skirt. He thought it was Nieves returning. Then the woman was fully illuminated, stopping five feet from him, and he saw that it was not Nieves. It was a woman different from any he had seen in the peons' quarters.

As Corado had said, most of these people were of Indian blood, and, while some like Maruca were decidedly attractive, it was the attraction of a vital young animal. They tended to flat, underslung hips and bandy legs, and their hair was coarse and straight as a horse's mane.

This one had none of that. Her beauty was striking in a buxom, peasant way. She was dressed in calico that must have come off one of the Boston brigs. Her hips made a ripe, flowing curve beneath the sleazy cloth; her breasts, beneath the square-cut bodice, were heavy and round. Her mass of hair was dark and wavy, and, though her eyes were dark, too, they had none of the bead-like

34

Indian quality he had seen. They were a deep coffee hue, with sultry little lights stirring through them, as she regarded him without speaking.

"If you've been talking with Maruca," he grinned, "I'm open for business."

"I haven't been talking with Maruca." Her Spanish had a strange accent to it.

"What's your name?"

"Aline."

"That isn't Spanish."

"My father named me."

"He was American?"

"Roger Bardine."

It took all the flippancy from him and wiped his grin off. He recalled Callahan's mention of Bardine's daughter. That explained the wave in her hair, the shape of her hips and thighs, but it didn't answer a dozen other things. He tried to bring his grin back again.

"Who was he?"

"You know who he was." She came to him, anger giving her lips a petulant shape. "He was the United States consul in California, and you've come to find him."

Her words went through him like a distinct shock, but this time he managed to hold his grin. "Honey, I'm just a lonely tar that got left behind when his ship sailed."

"You aren't," she said. "Captain Frémont was in the Salinas Valley a few months ago. He was supposed to be on some kind of scientific expedition. But I know he was hunting my father. And he didn't find him. I knew they would send someone else sooner or later. You're the man. Tell me you're the man."

He had the impulse to trust her, but caution bred of too many past betrayals made him play dumb. "I don't even know what you're talking about. Where do you come from?"

"I'm staying with my aunt and uncle at Rancho Atasco on the Little Sur. They took me in when my father disappeared. Uncle Luis came from town this afternoon and told us about you. I sneaked out the wagon and came over. I knew you were the one. You had to be. You're the only new American in Monterey for months." She caught his arm, speaking English now, an intense plea widening her eyes. "Please, please tell me you are the one. You don't know what it means to me. I'm so helpless. Nobody around here can help me. They are all so afraid. If I only knew someone was hunting my father, if I could only turn to someone for help. . . ."

It was a powerful plea. Her eyes were brimming with tears. Her full underlip was damp and glistening. She was so close her ripe breasts made a cushiony pressure against his chest. He knew that one word from him would relieve the heartaches, the worry, the desperation of months. And she looked so guileless, so badly in need of someone. Yet what if they had planted her on him? It was the oldest trick in the book. It had happened to him before. Rodríguez might be behind it. Her nearness sent a hot pulse through Hayward's throat, and he had to fight himself to keep from breaking, to play her along.

"You say everybody's afraid. Of what?"

"You know, you know," she said bitterly. "The *fantasmas* . . . the phantoms."

"Now what are you talking about? Who are they?"

"Who knows? I have never seen one of them. Few people have. But I saw a house they burned to the ground, once, and the bodies of the people they killed."

"They sound like bandits."

36

"Do bandits kill and burn and take no loot? Do bandits spirit a man away into thin air for nothing? I don't even know why they took my father. If they were holding him as a hostage, wouldn't they ask some kind of ransom?"

"Then who are they?"

"I told you, nobody knows. It is all just talk. My father thought it was some crazy peon revolting against the landholders. Colonel Archuleta claims it is some of the old diehards trying to win California back for Spain."

"That would be *Alcalde* Rodríguez. Didn't his family have some connection with the Spanish crown?"

She nodded. "My uncle suspects Rodríguez. He says you Yankees are getting strong here. The *fantasmas* are afraid of Yankee power, and that is why the *alcalde* closed the port to you. But Rodríguez himself claims he closed it because the *fantasmas* are really backed by Americans and led by an American trying to overthrow his rule here."

He grinned. "Phantoms in the night. How melodramatic!"

Her underlip took on a petulant shape. "Perhaps we are a melodramatic race. It is the people who named them. What would you call a band of murderers who are never seen?"

He chuckled ruefully. "You've got me."

Her face flushed with anger. "I see I have made a mistake. You cannot be a spy. You cannot be the one they sent after my father."

"I can't?"

"You do not take it seriously enough. It is a big joke. Everything is a big joke. You laugh all the time. You get drunk. You care nothing if people are suffering. They would not have trusted you on such a serious job. I am sorry I told you of the *fantasmas*."

37

"Who speaks of the *fantasmas?*"

It came in a roar, from down the lane. Both Hayward and Aline wheeled to see Corado coming toward them in his bowlegged, bear-like walk. They had been talking too intently to hear the rattle of his great cartwheel spurs. The rough, greasy texture of his cheeks was dark with anger. He caught Aline, swinging her back against the wall. His fist bunched her dress up so tightly that the edge of the bodice dug a deep crease into the soft upper swells of her breasts. She struggled to get free. "Let go, Miguel, you're hurting me."

"I'll hurt you more if you don't shut up about the *fantasmas*. I'm sick of everybody whining, sick of hearing about it. Who ever saw a *fantasma?* Not me. Not you. Not anybody. Just a bunch of old grandmothers whining around the fire and scaring everybody for nothing."

Hayward saw the pain contort Aline's face and grabbed the man's arm, trying to pull him free. "Let go. Can't you see you're hurting her?"

It was like trying to move a rock. Hayward hooked the man's elbow and put all his weight into it, jerking him violently away. Aline's dress ripped, exposing one of her heavy breasts, as Corado was wheeled around into Hayward. The man's face turned black with rage.

"*¡Chindago!*" he roared, and swung at Hayward.

Hayward blocked the blow, but the man's rush carried them both back into the wall. Corado came heavily against Hayward, kneeing him in the groin.

Hayward bent over with the sickening pain of it. All he could do was claw wildly for Corado's face. He caught a thumb in the man's mouth, yanked hard. He pulled the man off balance, and Hayward staggered into him. They both stumbled through the open door into the room.

38

Corado jerked free of the tearing thumb, his mouth bloody. Still sickened from the knee in the groin, Hayward lashed out with his shoe. The heavy brogan caught Corado viciously in the leg.

The man gasped and fell into Hayward. Grappling, they reeled across the room. Corado went heavily into the cone-shaped oven molded into the wall. Shouting with the pain of the hot adobe, he tried to twist free.

But Hayward had him pinned there, and jerked an arm free to slug the man. Blindly, Corado blocked the blow, then caught Hayward's arm again. At the same time he hooked his other elbow into Hayward's elbow. They grappled again, arm locked in arm, body pinned to body. And for the first time, Hayward was brought fully against the man's awesome strength.

He tried to tear his left arm free of that hooked elbow. It was like trying to escape a vise. He tried to jerk his right wrist out of Corado's fingers. It only seemed to grind the bones painfully together. Then Corado began to bear down.

Slowly, inexorably, he twisted Hayward back and down. Hayward gritted his teeth, groaning with the effort to keep the man from twisting him against the oven. The sweat ran down their faces like rain water. Their breathing made a husky roar in the room. Aline had followed them in and stopped halfway across the room, staring in horrified fascination.

Hayward might as well have tried to halt the turning of the earth. Gradually, with a popping of sinew, a cracking of bone, his body was twisted backward until he was bent against the oven instead of Corado. The heat of it burned through his shirt and stiffened him with pain.

Corado had not finished. With Hayward still straining to stop him, he kept twisting, slowly, inexorably, until Hayward was down on one knee. Then, with a sudden grunt, he let go of Hayward's right wrist and grabbed his hair.

Hayward tried to shift, tried to bring a blow into the man's face. But he was off balance, twisted backward on his knee. Corado threw all his weight on him, bearing him heavily onto his back on the floor. Hayward tried to slug at the man with his free fist, but Corado dodged the blow, jerking Hayward's head nearer the fire. Hayward struck again. But he had no leverage, and Corado only grunted with the blow. Hayward knew what was in the man's mind now. Aline did, too, for she stumbled across the room, pawing at Corado.

"Please, don't . . . not the fire!"

She could not move him. He lay sprawled on Hayward, rendering Hayward's struggles futile with his arm lock and his bear-like weight. His face was contorted with strain and anger. Corado yanked Hayward's head an inch nearer the fire. His voice, coming through clenched teeth, was a groan of rage.

"The *señorita* . . . she told me to keep him in his place, didn't she? It is time I do that. It is time I show him who's *amansador*. He'll remember as long as he lives."

Aline tore at his arm again. "No, Miguel, you can't!"

With a roar he let go of Hayward's head, caught her arm, spun her away. She went into the table so hard it upset, and she fell with it. Hayward tried to lunge up, but Corado blocked him with a shift of his weight. He caught the yellow hair again, and once more it was that inexorable straining of body against body, arm against arm, will against will.

And slowly, inexorably, Hayward's straining head was twisted into the flames. He could hear Aline sobbing as she lay huddled by the smashed table, could hear

Corado's stertorous breathing in his face, could feel the heat of the flames getting closer and closer.

And then his cheek was ground into the coals.

He shouted with searing pain. The insane strength of pure agony ran through his body. Even Corado's inexorable force was no match for it. Hayward's violent convulsion broke the man's grip momentarily. Before Corado could recover, Hayward heaved himself upward and threw him to one side. Then Hayward twisted over onto the man, turned into a raging animal by the pain.

He hit Corado in the face, and the man tried to roll away. He caught him and pulled him back and hit him again. Corado kicked him in the stomach and scrambled backward. Retching from the kick, Hayward crawled after him and lunged at him as he gained his feet.

Corado tried to block the blow, but he was off balance. It knocked him backward, and Hayward followed, hitting him in the face, in the belly, in the kidneys. Retreating and grunting sickly from the blows, Corado stumbled clear across the room, smashing into the wall.

His body was bent over and his face was slack from the shock of the blows. As Hayward lurched in to hit him again, Corado pulled himself away from the wall. Soddenly, Hayward brought a blow up from underneath, into the man's bent head. Corado took it full in the face and came on, butting Hayward in the belly.

He knocked Hayward back, and Hayward tripped on the wrecked table and fell flat on his back. Corado plunged after him, landing astraddle on all fours. He caught Hayward's hair in both hands, smashing his head brutally against the floor.

The whole world seemed to explode. Hayward tried to roll away. Corado dragged him back by his hair, slamming

41

his head against the floor again. Then he lifted Hayward's head up with one hand and slugged him in the face. He hit him again and again, shouting and roaring like some animal, until Hayward could hardly feel the shock of the blows and there was no fight left in him.

After a long time, Hayward realized the man's weight was gone. As from a great distance, he heard the panting, gasping breath, and then the voice.

"You going to get up?"

Hayward tried to move. He rolled over and tried to push himself up. But his arms would not support him, and he fell limply to the floor again. Everything was hazy, everything was pain, and he had no will left.

"I didn't think so," Corado panted. "I told you I was *amansador* here. Maybe now you know what that means."

Chapter Four

John Hayward spent a wretched night. Nieves put in most of it nursing his wounds with prickly-pear poultice and other native herbs, and feeding him Romero tea to quiet him down. The shock and pain finally wore off, and he slept. He woke early the next morning, stiff and sore, the cuts and bruises throbbing unmercifully. Nieves and El Sombrío were still asleep, snoring lustily, and Hayward rose and dressed. Each movement caused him to wince with pain, but nothing was broken.

He moved gingerly outside and found a bench against the wall, letting the heat of a rising sun bake out some of the hurt. His mind soon left the fight. There were too many other things to consider.

It had gone fast, almost too fast. Getting inland so soon, in such a good position to work from, finding Roger Bardine's daughter the first night. The progression had all seemed logical enough. And yet, he had actually found out nothing significant — with all his luck. Just a lot of pieces that did not fit together. And the fear. That was something he could not get over. Most of his Army career had consisted of undercover work. He had run up against plenty of secret political societies, terrorists, murderers who sought power over the people through fear. But their goals had usually been obvious; their activities followed some pattern; the motive behind their methods had been traceable. Rarely had he come up against such a universal fear caused by something so nebulous.

Dogs were stirring in the other dooryards, and a couple

43

of sleepy children peered from a window. El Sombrío came out, pulling on his shirt, blinking puffy eyes.

"Looks like a hot summer. All our horses will get heated up running the cattle and die."

"I never saw such a cheerful cuss," Hayward said.

El Sombrío squinted at his marred face. "Aline said that was a great fight. I wish I had seen it."

"Why is Corado so touchy about the *fantasmas?*"

El Sombrío stared owl-eyed at him. "You still talk about that after last night?"

"Corado isn't around. I should at least know why I got the beating."

El Sombrío glanced furtively over his shoulder, then came closer, speaking in husky confidence. "I will tell you once, and then we will not speak of it again. Corado is like a child, one minute sunshine, the next a storm. One never knows when he will explode, or why. But I know he is sick of this *fantasma* business. Men are deserting from all the big ranches in fear of what the *fantasmas* have done or may do. Last year Don Fernando Mateo, Carlota's father, was killed at a bear fight. It looked like an accident, but they found out later it wasn't. Everybody said it was the *fantasmas,* and many of our best riders began to desert. It is getting harder and harder for Corado to run the ranch. What men are left will not go into the mountains after horses, will not do this, will not do that. And now it is said that Don Antonio is also marked for death."

"Don Antonio?"

"The son of Don Fernando, the *Señorita* Carlota's brother."

"But why should he be marked? Why should they kill Don Fernando?"

"Who knows? Perhaps the old man knew too much." El

44

Sombrío's voice grew husky. "Perhaps he was a *fantasma*."

"Have you ever seen a *fantasma?*"

The old man's face turned gray. He withdrew from Hayward. There was a haunted light to his eyes. Hayward had seen the same light in the eyes of Negroes facing a voodoo *mamaloi* down in New Orleans, or the eyes of a Tarahumure Indian when Montezuma and the sacred fires at Pecuris were mentioned. He realized that El Sombrío and the rest of these people were no different than the other primitive peoples he had known. When they met something they did not understand, it immediately entered the realm of superstition and witchcraft, and made their fear blind.

Hayward chuckled, slapping El Sombrío affectionately on the back. "All right, Gloomy One. I will not disturb your devils further. Let's go in and have some of that breakfast I smell cooking."

Nieves clucked around him like a mother hen, and it was all Hayward could do to keep her from feeding him. After breakfast, El Sombrío told Hayward that Corado wanted them both at the corrals.

Dust hung thickly over the shadowy pattern of pens, and the compound was filled with the shouts of men and the squeal of animals. As Hayward and the old man approached, they saw two people coming from the main house, beyond the corrals, followed by a fat old woman in black and a half dozen chattering servants. One of those in the lead was Carlota Mateo. She did not wear the Spanish comb and mantilla, the voluminous silk skirt of yesterday. Her hair was still upswept, but was piled into the crown of a flat-topped hat set piquantly on the back of her head. She wore a white silk shirtwaist and a fancy green coat, and a heavy riding skirt of fawn-colored buckskin. Beside her was a tall young man in his early twenties, dressed in

45

a flamboyant jacket of red velvet and blue silk that was covered with gilt frogs and silver buttons.

"That is Antonio Mateo," El Sombrío said.

Hayward saw the band of black crêpe on the man's sleeve that was the mark of mourning for his father. He had a sensitive face, a little pale compared with most of his countrymen. There was an intense aristocracy to the aquiline nose, the effeminate lips, the delicately cleft chin. He held a pair of doeskin gloves in one hand, tugging nervously at them and frowning at Carlota. The fat woman in black was hurrying to keep up with them, wringing her hands and crossing herself and pleading with Carlota.

"Please, little one, do not do this foolish thing. It is dangerous out in those mountains . . . bears and wolves, wild Indians, tempests . . . remember what happened to your father . . . !"

"We will not talk of that, my good aunt," Carlota said. "If Corado cannot keep his men on the ranch, I want to know why. And the only way to find out, apparently, is to go out with them." She stopped speaking as she saw Hayward. Then she veered toward him, slapping her quirt against the buckskin riding skirt. She stopped before Hayward, unsmiling. "Antonio, this is the American who has come to serve his sentence here. Juan Hayward."

Antonio Mateo met Hayward's eyes haughtily. His lips pinched together, and he flicked his gloves disdainfully at some dust that didn't show on his jacket. "I understand Corado showed you your place last night," he said. "You will keep it, and will not speak unless spoken to."

Hayward felt the blood rise in his cheeks. But before he could respond, Carlota dismissed him with a toss of her head and walked on down to the corrals, calling imperiously for Corado. He came running like a squat, bow-

46

legged bear from a group at one of the corrals.

"I am going with you," she said. "Saddle up that black you have been working."

Corado was sweating heavily. He pushed his long black hair out of his eyes, shaking his head. "*Patrona*, this trip is not for you."

"Do not give me orders," she said angrily. "I'm sick of being told what to do. Are you going to get me that horse, or would you like to spend a week in the stocks?"

Corado looked helplessly at Antonio, but the young man gave him a frozen smile and did not speak. Then Corado turned back to Carlota. After seeing him roaring and brawling with the other woman, it was almost comical to see how different he was before this one. His perplexity made him almost childish. Like a sycophantic innkeeper, he rubbed his hands and shrugged his shoulders.

"If you must go, not the black horse. I told you how he was."

"And I told you to stop giving me orders. I have had my eye on that black horse ever since you got him, and you've had plenty of time to gentle him. I give you one more chance, Corado. My patience is at an end."

Again the man's eyes shot helplessly about the group. But none could offer him help. Wiping the sweat from his face with the hairy back of a hand, he turned and got one of the ropes hanging on the corral. Then he stepped into the pen, maneuvering a black horse out of a bunch milling against the fence. He blocked it off in a corner and put the rope on it with a casual skill. Then he led it out, prancing and snorting. There was a savage look to its bloodshot eyes, and Hayward saw a lot of outlaw in the way it fought the rope. Corado hitched one end of the rawhide line about its nose, then slapped it hard on the rump. The horse squealed angrily and bolted. When it had run thirty feet, Corado dug his heels in and snubbed his end of the rope across his hip. It stopped the horse sharply, snapping its head around with a loud pop.

"He'll break its neck," Hayward said.

"Ah, no," El Sombrío chuckled. "You have much to learn of how a *californio* handles his mounts. That is to limber him up for early riding."

Corado walked down the rope to the fiddling, snorting horse and slapped its rump again. The animal ran once more, and once more Corado snubbed it down, snapping its neck on the other side.

"That should take the stiffness out," El Sombrío said. "He will run smooth as oil now."

Another man brought up a heavy rig. As they threw it on the excited black, Hayward saw that it was a fancy sidesaddle. His coffee-colored brow still corrugated with that worried frown, Corado turned toward Carlota. Snapping her quirt against her skirt, she went to the horse. The man held a stirrup while she toed it. As she swung up, the horse pitched wildly. She was thrown belly down across the saddle, with but one foot in the stirrup. She grabbed wildly for the reins, shouting at Corado.

"Let him go! I can handle him, if you'll only let him go."

Corado hung onto the bridle, face contorted. "I'm afraid to. He'll kill you."

His weight on the bridle swung the horse like a pendulum as it bucked, and the violent motion threw Carlota away. Her skirt caught on the saddle horn as she slid off, and there was a sharp rip. She hit hard, and a dozen of them were around her in a minute. Corado let go of the black and ran to the group, tearing the servants and riders

48

aside to reach her. Hayward saw that she had already rolled over and was getting to her feet. Her skirt had been ripped to the waist, and he had a momentary glimpse of alabaster thighs before she angrily pulled it together. Her eyes were blazing with rage as she turned on Corado.

"You did that on purpose! You wanted me pitched so I wouldn't go with you!"

Corado held his hands as if praying. "*Patrona*, I didn't. I swear I didn't."

"If you hadn't held on, I could have stopped him."

"But you weren't even in the saddle. If I had let go, he would have carried you right into the fence."

"Don't contradict me!" she cried. She was still gripping the heavy quirt, and she brought it up and lashed Corado across the face in a fit of uncontrollable rage. "I am sick of your blocking me at every turn. I am sick of your drunks in town and your tawdry love affairs and your stupid boasting." She struck him again, driving him back. "Get out of my sight, you filthy Indian."

He stopped backing up suddenly. The whiplashes formed two livid stripes, gradually filling with blood, across his flat nose, his swarthy cheeks. His eyes were twitching and watering and squinted shut with pain. But he did not raise his hands to his face. Gradually his twitching eyes opened. And Hayward saw the change that had come to him. He was no longer a dog jumping through the hoop for an adored mistress. His face was filled with that same stark, primitive savagery Hayward had seen the first time Carlota had berated him from the coach, down in Monterey. Only now the shining eyes were strangely blank, like a pair of opaque beads, staring at her. It was a look that went back to the primitive sources of the man, back ten thousand years, and it was something Carlota could not touch.

Hayward saw the rage leave her face for an instant. Her lips parted, and her eyes grew dark and luminous, like a child's, looking into a dark room. Then the anger gripped her again. With an inarticulate sound, she wheeled away and stamped off toward the house, blinking back tears of rage and humiliation. Corado did not move. He stood there, arms dangling, with the blood slowly oozing from the cuts on his face, staring after her.

"She should not have done that," El Sombrío whispered. "She should not have called him an Indian."

Antonio Mateo shook his immaculate gloves at the riders and the servants. "Very well, it's all over now. Go back to the house and get your horses together." He turned to Corado. "Get Nieves to fix your face up and then come back. We won't let this little upset keep us from our trip."

Corado did not answer. Hayward saw that he was trembling. His whole body was trembling. Antonio snapped his glove impatiently at the man.

"Corado, do you hear me?"

Corado wheeled, without looking at Antonio, and walked over to the corral fence. He stood with his back to them, one hand on a fence bar, his head bowed. Hayward saw that he was still trembling. Antonio waited a moment, frowning at the man, then went to him, speaking in a low voice.

"I understand how humiliating that was to you, before all your people, Corado, and I shall speak to my sister about it. But you know her. You know she will be over it tomorrow and will probably apologize for it, might even let you have another weekend in town. We can't hold it against her. She's a proud and temperamental girl."

"I do not hold it against her," Corado said. The words stopped Antonio, with a surprised look coming to his face.

50

Corado turned, holding his hand to the wounds now. The primitive rage was gone. His voice was thick and husky. "She is just a little girl, isn't she? Just like something wild that has never been tamed, isn't she? Like a horse or something." He tried to grin. "That is it. And who can blame a horse that has never been tamed? Someday a man will come along and break her, won't he? But until then she will go on whipping me and pushing me around and treating me like a big puppy her papa gave her. I guess I do not mind. She is my *patrona,* and I do not mind. But someday a man will tame her, won't he?" Corado dropped his hand from his face, squinting at Antonio, his voice growing more strident. "That is true, isn't it? Someday a man will tame her?"

"Of course, Corado, of course. Now go up and get something on that face. We will try to leave before she gets on fresh clothes. She is a stubborn one and might still try to go with us."

Corado turned to El Sombrío. "Mix some gunpowder with that tallow in the bucket by the corral gate. It will do to rub in the cuts." He broke off as he saw Hayward, and the humiliation rose in the surface of his face again. Then he laughed self-consciously. "You saw a joke, my friend. Last night I whipped you. This morning a woman whips me." He took off his bandanna, holding it to the cuts, and walked to Hayward, slapping him on the back. "I knew you had the makings of a man who could be my *compadre,* Juanito. Not another in all California could stand on his own two feet the morning after he fought with me."

"I thought you'd be angry," Hayward said.

"Angry? Who is angry?" His humor was still a self-conscious effort. "I told you. Wenching and drinking and fighting. What else is there in life? And when have I had

51

such a fight as last night? You were like ten men. It will be good to have you with us this morning."

"You are taking him?" Antonio asked.

"Why not?" Corado said expansively. "I saw him ride yesterday. And he has the courage of the bear. He will be a good one to have along. We have a hard enough time finding men who will go into those mountains. Show him how you can ride, Juanito. Rope a horse out of the pen, Sombrío."

The old man had brought up the bucket of tallow and a handful of black powder. He poured the powder into Corado's hand. While Corado mixed some tallow with it and rubbed it into his cuts, El Sombrío roped out a roan for Hayward. They saddled and bridled the horse, and Hayward stepped on. It began pitching, and he rode it around a couple of circles before it spilled its morning vinegar and settled down. It wasn't much of a show, but it pleased Corado.

Antonio looked at him suspiciously. "Where does a sailor learn to ride like that?"

"I spent a little time in Mexico," Hayward said.

He didn't tell him that when he was only sixteen he had trained at the Colegio Militar in Mexico City, competing with some of the best cavalrymen in the world. He didn't tell him how many countless weeks you spent on a bareback horse when you signed up with the cavalry at West Point. He didn't tell him how many pitching bronchos he'd ridden out when he was buying the horses for Leavenworth. Maybe the Army didn't teach a man cattle work, but, when it was through with a cavalryman, he could ride with anybody in the world.

The other men had all gathered their saddle strings now and were waiting restlessly to go. One of them roped

52

out a handsome chestnut for Antonio and put aboard a richly mounted saddle, stamped in green and gold and glittering with silver plating. Corado stepped aboard his fretting black and put the spurs to it, and they all smoked out in a haze of dust.

They headed west, across the meadows and into the mountains, a half dozen riders followed by the *remuda* of spare horses hazed along by a couple of youths. They dipped into a deep valley, riding through wild oats so tall Hayward could not see over it. They flushed antelope and heard the bellow of wild blackhorns without ever catching sight of them. Sometime before noon Corado reined up for a moment and pointed to the tracks of a bear on the ground.

"I wish we had time to catch him," Antonio said. "Monterey has not had a good bull and bear fight in a long time."

Then his face darkened, and Hayward knew he was thinking of his father.

They penetrated deeper into the mountains. It was a country of lonely grandeur, with something almost passionate to its savage beauty. Hayward had rarely seen such rugged mountains. The slopes were so steep and precipitous that it sometimes took the men hours to cover a few miles. The cañons were like deep and twisted wounds, so deep in some places that their shadowed bottoms were hidden to the eye. The timber was dense, with the tremendous redwoods towering like giants above all else and seeming to scrape the sky. Hayward had the feeling of intense isolation, of being lost in the hidden heart of a land known to few men.

They dismounted a few minutes for a lunch of jerky and cold coffee carried in gum-pitched *morrales* slung from sad-

53

dle horns. Then they rode again, crossing the Sacramento River in late afternoon. The Sierras were within sight now, rising blue and misty beyond orchards of peach and apple.

Born and bred to the saddle, these leathery *vaqueros* of the Rancho del Sur showed little exhaustion when they made night camp in a cañon where the wind howled like a demon. Again it was jerked meat and coffee, heated this time over an open fire. They sat around, smoking and talking in soft Spanish voices after the meal. Hayward was becoming acquainted with some of the other men by now. There was Pío Tico, a narrow, enigmatic youth with a face that might have been carved from mahogany. He was the *jinete*, the broncho breaker of the ranch, and felt the honor of the station keenly. And there was Nicolás, who played the guitar and sang sad love songs and said he had never had a woman. And Gregorio, who entered little into the comradeship of the others, sitting like a statue by the fire and staring into the outer darkness.

They awoke next morning to find the cañon shrouded in a thick fog. Gingko trees and marestail and carpets of gilas and mariposas appeared abruptly out of the morning fog, swirling like milky serpents about the horses' hoofs. They rode through it till almost noon, before the sun finally broke through. Hayward could hear a distant roar, and Corado told him they were near enough to the coast to hear the surf.

At last, they came upon a spring, at the foot of a sharply rising slope, and Pío Tico found the fresh tracks of horses that had recently watered there. They pushed on and soon sighted the band, grazing on the slope.

"We are at the mouth of Higuera Cañon," Antonio said. "If we run them in there, they will be trapped."

"But it is twenty miles long," Corado protested. "We

might have to run them all day. Why not go up onto the mesa and toward the sea?"

"And lose them over the cliffs?"

"That is what will stop them. They are too smart to run off the edge."

"No horse is smart when he is stampeding," Antonio said. "I say the cañon."

"And I say the mesa."

"Are you arguing with me, too?"

"But, *patrón*. . . ."

"Don't contradict me. I am beginning to think Carlota was right. Those are my orders, Corado. We run the horses up the cañon."

Corado turned dark under the rebuke. He met the man's smoldering eyes for a moment, lips working, as if to speak again. But the anger was mounting too obviously in Antonio's pale face, and Corado wheeled his black sharply and waved the crew down the slope. The two horse wranglers held the spare animals back while the others fanned out and approached the mustangs warily. Hayward followed Antonio, watching heads pop up one by one as the grazing mustangs caught their scent.

The band began drifting toward the mouth of the cañon with the leader circling around the flanks. He was a magnificently muscled buckskin, nipping at flanks and shoulders to keep the younger stallions in line. The sight of him made Antonio lose his hauteur.

"Look at that leader," he said. "We've tried to trap him before. Did you ever see such a magnificent rump? He would have a jump-off like a jack rabbit."

"Good roper," Hayward said.

Antonio glanced back at him, seeming to realize how he had let down his reserve. "What would you know about roping?" he asked thinly. He gigged his horse away without waiting for a reply.

Hayward tried to be mad and couldn't. There was something almost pathetic about the young man's effort at sarcasm, like a kid trying to be tough.

They pushed the horses into the cañon. Then Corado sent Pío Tico and Gregorio to get ahead of the band, so they would have the mustangs between two groups of riders. But the cañon narrowed to a steep-walled gorge. Every time the pair tried to flank the band and get in front, the wily leader blocked them off and darted ahead. It seemed to justify Corado's earlier claim, and he kept sending Antonio black looks. But Antonio would say nothing. They followed the horses like that into the afternoon, penetrating miles into the wild and tumbled gorge, failing in every attempt to get ahead of the band. Corado was growing nervous as a spooked broncho, riding back and forth, looking at the cliffs above, arguing that they should drop away and let the band drift back into the open.

Then a spur cañon opened up ahead of the mustangs, and Antonio waved at it, shouting: "That is probably a dead end. Gregorio, Sombrío, on their flank, turn them!"

With a shout, the pair ran for the flank, veering the mustangs. Then the others started popping quirts against their rawhide leggings and spurring their animals into a run. The startled mustangs headed straight for the mouth of the spur. In the squeal of animals, the din of rattling rocks and pounding hoofs, the other sound came to Hayward like the thin crack of a whip.

He saw Antonio stiffen in the saddle, mouth torn wide with shock. Then the man pitched off his horse. Still not realizing what had happened, Hayward wheeled his mount. Gregorio and Sombrío had already pulled up and were

56

jumping down, fumbling pistols from their saddlebags, firing toward the cliffs above.

Hayward ran his horse to Antonio, jumped off. There was a bullet hole in Antonio's white shirt, rapidly filling with blood. Hayward went to one knee, helped the dazed man to sit up. Corado had joined them by then, swinging off his lathered black. Antonio clutched Hayward with one hand, his voice shrill with pain and hysteria.

"Now who's crazy? Now who says the phantoms in the night are a fairy story? Get after them, Corado. They tried to kill me, just like they killed my father. Don't stand there gaping, get after them."

"*Patrón*, your wound . . . ?"

"El Sombrío will take care of that. Get after those murderers. It came from the cliff up there. If you return without their heads, I'll have a new *amansador* on Rancho del Sur."

Hayward saw the sweat break from the pores on Corado's face, saw his nostrils splay out and flutter like those of an enraged horse. But he wheeled his black and galloped for the slope, waving his arm for Gregorio and Pío Tico to follow. Hayward mounted and spurred his horse after them. It had happened so fast he still didn't get all the implications, but he sensed he was close to something he shouldn't lose. Corado did not tell him to turn back, and the four of them forced their squealing mounts up the steep slope to the base of the rocky cliffs. They had to detour till they found a defile that led through the ramparts and to the mesa above. Here Corado reined up, surly as a bear, growling to himself.

"That old woman! Why did he come if he thinks they are out to kill him? *Fantasmas en la noche*. Who ever heard anything so crazy? Probably some Indian that had

57

this bunch of mustangs all staked out and got mad when we jumped them first."

"Would an Indian have a gun?" Pío Tico asked. He was off his horse and circling through the rocks, and finally he stopped and crouched down. "Here are his tracks. They come from the south. He went back over that ridge behind the mesa."

Still grumbling and cursing, Corado spurred his lathered, blowing horse once more, and they raced across the mesa and into the timber. They had to slow down here, picking their way through the dense pine and cypress. At the top they halted, with a view of the country beyond spread out beneath them. They studied the slopes and ridges that undulated away into the afternoon haze. It was Hayward who finally saw the flash of movement, west of them, climbing the next slope. They put the spurs to their horses again, fighting the steep, densely timbered slopes. Hayward had never seen such up-and-down riding. They topped another ridge but could no longer see the movement or a rider ahead. Pío Tico said he could not have turned back without their seeing him, so he must be going on to the coast. They pushed down out of the high country onto a mesa that overlooked the sea. The roar of the surf seemed to shake the land. They reached a great cliff with a soupy fog swirling at its base, half hiding the immense breakers battering themselves against the black rocks below.

"I know," Corado said sarcastically. "He sprouted wings and flew off."

"He must have turned either north or south," Pío Tico said. "Let us hunt for tracks."

They circled half an hour without finding any sign, and finally Corado quit in disgust. "We might as well go back."

"Are you crazy?" Pío Tico asked. "The way Don Anto-

58

nio feels now, he will have our hides whipped from us if we come back empty-handed."

Corado grew dark with rage. "I am *amansador* here. I say we have gone far enough on this fool's errand. There is too much work to do at the ranch to waste our time hunting down some Indian who didn't want us to get his horses."

Pío Tico shook his head. "I think you are wrong."

With a curse, Corado reined his horse savagely against the man and struck him backhand across the face, knocking Pío Tico violently from the saddle. He sprawled on his back on the ground, so dazed he could not rise for a moment. Finally he got to his feet, wiping the blood from his lips. His face shone with sweat, looking like some dark and polished wood. The whites of his eyes gleamed in startling contrast as he stared at Corado. His voice shook hoarsely when he spoke.

"You will do that once too often, Corado. If Don Antonio found out you forced me to disobey him, he would have you killed. You know he would."

Corado did not have as tight a leash on his rage as Pío Tico. His face turned black with it, and his nostrils fluttered, and the muscles bunched into little knots down the length of his clenched jaw. For a moment Hayward thought he would explode. Then he shouted: "Fools! Chicken-hearted scum! The old woman says one word, and you are like coyotes."

He jerked his horse around so hard it squealed with pain, and then raked it cruelly with his spurs, making it leap and head across the mesa at a dead run. Hayward watched him go, letting out a relieved sigh.

"For a moment I thought he was going to kill you."

Pío Tico bent to pick up his hat, slapping the dust

from it against his greasy leggings. "In California, my friend, the *patrón* is next to God. Even Corado dares not go against the word of Don Antonio." He turned to look north, letting the anger and humiliation settle, finally speaking again. "It is not likely that the man we follow went that way. There are too many steep cañons. Let us look to the south for the tracks."

Chapter Five

They rode south along the cliffs, with the sea snarling about the rocks below and the fog rising slowly till it began to shroud the riders. It was clammy and chill and made Hayward shiver, even in his heavy coat. But Pío Tico was determined not to return empty-handed.

They crossed more mesas that ran back a few hundred yards to be met by the sheer walls of the steep and impassable mountains. Night was falling, and the fog was like a pearly cloak over the land when they reached the cañon that cut through the mesa and opened out onto a rocky beach far below.

"This is the mouth of Higuera Cañon," Pío Tico said. "It is where the mustangs would have reached if they'd kept running."

"Then we're near our own camp," Hayward said.

"Farther than you think. The cañon twists like a snake. It would take us a day of riding to get back to Don Antonio by following it. The way we came is quicker."

Gregorio stirred in his saddle, pointing into the depths. They all strained to see, until they caught the wink of a light. It looked like a campfire. Gregorio began fingering his face and pouting his lips.

"Maybe we better get more men."

A varnish of excitement made Pío Tico's eyes shine. "Don't be a fool. It would take us till tomorrow. Are you so afraid?"

That look came into Gregorio's face, the same look Hayward had seen in El Sombrío's face, the mingling of superstitious awe and fear. "It might be that these are not ordinary men, Pío Tico," he said in a hushed voice. "It might be that these are the *fantasmas*."

"Then you have your choice," Pío Tico said. "This . . . or the wrath of Antonio Mateo."

Gregorio's face turned ashen. He sat his fiddling horse for a minute, staring down into the rapidly darkening cañon. Then, without a word, he swung down. Pío Tico dismounted also, pulling a pair of brass-mounted pistols from his saddlebags, a handful of lead balls, a buckskin of powder. He studied Hayward a moment, then handed him one of the pistols.

"You have come with us this far. You deserve it."

Grinning, Hayward accepted the heavy gun, pulled his shirt pocket open to take the powder Pío Tico poured out, then accepted the four lead balls the man gave him. They spent precious moments seeking a trail that the horses could follow down. Unable to find one, they finally bunched the animals and began the precarious descent on foot.

It was hard going. Once Hayward tripped and slid down twenty feet of talus before a mat of scrub oak stopped him. The rest of the way down was through matted madroña and oak and vines that gave them plenty of handholds. At the bottom they had more dense underbrush to claw their way through. As they drew closer to the illumination, they saw it was not a campfire but a row of lighted windows. From beyond that a horse whinnied softly, and then they heard the low hum of voices. Stealthily the three men crept closer through the brush. Then foliage crackled sharply against Hayward's shoulder. Several of the horses ahead whinnied and began stamping and pulling at their lines.

Someone shouted from within the building. In that last

62

instant before the light went out, Hayward launched himself in a headlong run for the building. Then there was a crash of breaking glass as someone within the house knocked a lamp to the floor, and the windows suddenly went black. Hayward did not think he had ever been in such blackness.

He ran blindly into the wall. It stunned him, and his clawing hands found a corner. There was more shouting from within, a wild squeal from a horse, as Hayward stumbled around the corner. He ran solidly into a pair of men coming out the door. They knocked him backward, with one of them coming up against him. The man struck for his belly. Hayward took the blow, gasping with pain, and whipped wildly at the man with his pistol.

He felt the impact of iron on bone, and the man fell away.

The other had tried to veer aside. Hayward wheeled and ran at the sound of his pounding boots, clawing blindly for him. He caught the man's heavy coat for an instant. But the man tore free, and Hayward lost him in the utter darkness.

There was more shouting and the sound of a struggle somewhere on Hayward's flank. "Tico?" he shouted.

"Over here," Pío Tico answered. His voice did not come from the direction of the fight. Hayward was running toward the sound, when another man, rushing from the door, crossed his path and spilled him flat. Hayward rolled over with more shouting in his ears and then the angry drum of hoofs. As he came to his feet, the brush of the cañon crashed and boomed with the headlong passage of many horses. He stood there, panting for breath, helplessly listening to the sounds die away.

He realized he was still holding a button and some of the cloth he had torn from the man's coat, and stuffed it absently in his pocket. From his right, Pío Tico's voice came again.

"Is it safe to light a match?"

"I think they're all gone."

The man struck a light and carried it inside, finding a lamp. He lit it and brought it out. The glass hurricane cover had been shattered, but the brass container was still intact, and the exposed wick sputtered peevishly in the cañon breeze. Its yellow light bloomed over a man on the ground. It was the one Hayward had pistol whipped, lying sprawled on his face. Pío Tico's voice held sharp surprise. "An American."

He was six feet tall and broad as a house, with a beard that spread like red hoarfrost over his whole chest. Hayward saw it wasn't the one whose coat he had torn, for this man wore no coat. He had a buckskin shirt and elkhide leggings black with grease. And on his feet, beaded and fringed, were a pair of moccasins.

Gregorio came in out of the darkness, and they dragged the man inside. It was an adobe building, littered with the gear of a long stay. There were pack saddles piled in a corner, some of them empty, some bulging with the swarthy pelts of beaver and otter. Clothes were littered everywhere, a pair of blue jeans and a white shirt lying in a heap in the corner, more elkhide leggings drying over a fire that had been kicked out. There were a couple of red blankets in a corner. Hayward walked to them, separating them with a toe.

"Hudson's Bay four-pointers," he said. "Look more like trade blankets. They haven't been used."

The red-bearded man was regaining consciousness now. He rolled over, rubbing the back of his head, blinking in the light. He had a broad, leathery face, his mouth almost hidden in the brier patch of his beard. His pale blue eyes were set deeply in pouched lids, bloodshot with heavy drinking. They regarded each man with a sly twinkle that held more speculation than anger.

"*¿Habla español?*" Pío Tico asked.

"Not much," the man said.

"We'll talk English, then," Hayward said. "Who are you?"

"What's it to you?" blustered the man. He got heavily to his feet, speaking in a hoarse voice. "What right you got busting in here, clunking a man on the head, scaring all his horses away?"

"We were on the trail of a man who tried to kill one of us," Hayward stated flatly.

The man frowned at him, then squinted one eye judiciously. "Must have been that Injun."

"What Indian?"

"Some Injun hit here in the afternoon. His horse was lathered. He was mad as a bear in a cave. We didn't speak his lingo, but we made out with signs. Seemed he'd been staking out a band of mustangs for two or three days, and then this crew from over the mountains jumped them before he could do anything."

"He was the one who shot at us?" Hayward asked.

"I don't know about that," the man muttered. "But he was hopping mad."

Hayward turned to Pío Tico, reverting to Spanish. "Looks like Corado might have been right. This one says an Indian blew in here this afternoon, mad about those mustangs we jumped." He glanced back at the red-bearded man. "You still haven't said who you are."

The man did not seem quite so mad now. "A trapper, my friend. James Morgan, come in from Salt Lake, come

65

in from Jackson Hole, come in over the biggest desert and the tallest mountains you ever set peepers on."

"Not just you."

"I guess there was more than one of us."

"Why should the others take off like that?"

Morgan glanced at Pío Tico, pursed his lips, then looked back at Hayward. "We heard the *alcalde* had closed the country to Yankees. But we was doing so good with the furs we hated to leave, poaching or not. We thought you were some soldiers from Monterey."

"We're not. This is part of the crew from Rancho del Sur. I got left behind when my brig sailed, and they tossed me in jail. I'm serving out my time at the ranch."

"A sailor?" Morgan's laugh was like a belch. "I wager you do them a lot of good." Then he sobered. "They ain't going to pull me in, are they?"

Hayward turned to Pío Tico, repeating in Spanish what the man had said. "You believe his story?"

Pío Tico was frowning at the man's feet. "I would not, except for his moccasins. When we reached the top of the cliffs at the spot from which Don Antonio was shot, I saw the tracks the gunman left. They were of the wing boot, such as my people wear, and certainly not moccasins like this."

"Then we really have nothing to hold him for."

Pío Tico shook his head reluctantly. "I would like someone to take back. But we have no proof against this one, and Don Antonio could legally do nothing to him. It would only infuriate Don Antonio more to get a man he could not vent some of his rage on in punishment."

Hayward glanced at Morgan again. He was still suspicious of the man. He knew if he told Pío Tico about the fur poaching, they would probably turn Morgan over to

66

Alcalde Rodríguez, and Rodríguez would throw him in jail. But that wouldn't do Hayward any good.

He told Morgan: "They aren't going to take you."

"Thanks for helping me," Morgan said.

"Maybe it wasn't exactly help. There's an old proverb in Mexico. A wolf out of the trap sometimes goes back to the pack."

The man was still grinning, but a sly twinkle ran through his blue eyes. "Now what could you mean by that?"

Chapter Six

Pío Tico doubted that the men with the mustangs would wait for them to return, so they headed straight through the mountains for the ranch. It took them two days, and they reached the ranch on the afternoon of the second day. Dust hung like a haze of golden meal over the corrals, and the sultry air rang with the squeal of angry horses, the shouts of men, and the stutter of hoofs.

As they approached, Hayward saw Corado with a group of men at the big breaking corral. The *amansador* caught sight of the three approaching and turned, waiting for them. His legs were spread, his shoulders sloping, his face sullen. Both Pío Tico and Gregorio slowed down, glancing uncomfortably at each other.

"Come on, you *bribónes*," Corado yelled. "The worst I can do is hang you."

They drew their horses to a halt before him, and Hayward saw that there was no real anger in his face. "I thought you'd be fit to have our hides," he said.

Corado spat into the dust. "If Don Antonio had taken it out on me, when I got back, maybe I'd pass it on to you. But he was already so drunk he didn't even remember what happened."

They told him what they had found in the mountains.

He frowned, rubbing sweat off his chin. "I told you it was just some Indian. One of you better go tell Don Antonio. He wanted to know, and I don't dare disobey any more of his orders, even if he is too drunk to remember." Corado saw Pío Tico and Gregorio look surreptitiously at each other, and swore hoarsely. "Not you two. I need Pío Tico to bust that buckskin we got in the mountains. He's been falling back on every *jinete* that tops him, and nobody can stop him. You tell Don Antonio, Hayward. Maybe he will not be so hard on you."

Hayward saw Pío Tico turn away and leer and knew they expected him to get the brunt of Antonio's rage. Yet he wanted a chance to talk with the man, and, if Antonio was drunk, something valuable might come out. It was worth a chance.

A servant answered his knock at the recessed door of the big sprawling house, and he was ushered into a gloomy living room. There were slot-like windows with sills three feet deep, guarded by iron gratings that threw their barred shadow pattern across the black and white Indian blankets that were used for rugs. At one end of the long room was a vast fireplace with a foot-high adobe hearth pitted for a half-dozen pot fires. On the hand-hewn mantel were a pair of ancient Spanish helmets and a battered cuirass that must have been handed down through the family from the time of Cortés. Before the hearth sat Antonio Mateo, sprawled in a great high-backed chair, a decanter and glass on the table beside him. His eyes were puffy and bloodshot in his fragile face. A rumpled, drink-stained shirt was pulled awkwardly over the bandage on his left shoulder. He blinked at Hayward, finally recognized him, sneered.

"Well, the intrepid adventurers have returned. Empty-handed, I do not doubt."

Hayward went over to him and told him what they had found, watching carefully for the effects on the man's face. He saw the man's thin brows raise at the name of James Morgan.

"You know him?" Hayward asked.

"An American trapper," Antonio said petulantly. "He caused some trouble in Monterey a few months ago, got away before Rodríguez could imprison him. What's the difference? You didn't get them." He flung his hand out, knocking the glass off the table. "They are still out there, waiting, waiting for me just the way they waited for my father." His voice grew shrill and strident. "And someday, when I am like this, I will forget. That's why I do this. To forget. A man cannot ride around day and night with that on his soul. He has to lose it somehow. And someday I will forget, and I will wander out alone, and. . . ." He broke off sharply, staring up at Hayward in something close to surprise. Then he settled back, his bloodshot eyes glazed. His lips formed the words slackly. "You think I am a coward, don't you?"

"I hate to judge a man. . . ."

"A coward, a whining, puling milksop, good for nothing but serenading the ladies and spending his drunken nights afraid of his shadow, living in dread of nothing but a myth, nothing but a fairy story used by mothers to frighten their babies."

"Suppose I don't think it's a myth," Hayward said. "Suppose I believe you have good cause to fear."

Antonio gazed at him a moment, mouth slack and wet. At last he said: "Why do you say that?"

Hayward walked to the foot-high hearth, took a seat. "I have seen the fear in your people. It would take something very ugly to cause that. There doesn't seem to be anything you can pin down, but. . . ."

"Who can pin nothing down? What about my father? He was killed, wasn't he? It was last year. He had gone on a bear hunt, as is a custom among us. We rope the bear and drag him into town to fight with a bull. My father's rope

70

broke. The bear attacked him and killed him. El Sombrío showed me the rope. It was not frayed. It had not broken by itself. Somebody had cut it almost through."

"Why should someone want him dead?"

"Someone? You say someone?" Antonio rose sharply, almost upsetting himself. Then he walked around the table, placing a hand on it with each step for support. "Why not say the name? Are we that afraid of it? The *fantasmas*. They killed him. We all know they killed him."

"But why?"

"Perhaps he knew too much. He would not take me into his confidence. He thought me weak and irresponsible and totally hopeless. But I know this much. My father thought the *fantasmas* were a band of bandits, robbers, plunderers, led by a peon with some crazy dream of empire. He thought they were gathering, slowly, waiting until they had enough strength to overthrow the government and take command. That's why it is all so shadowy. They have not shown themselves yet. They are not ready to strike. Once in a while somebody finds out who they are, or recognizes one of them, and is killed. But that is all. Just somebody killed, or somebody disappearing, a moment of violence in the shadows without any reason or any answer."

"That's what makes it so mysterious to the people."

"Of course. They see no plunder taken, no politics involved, no reason for what has occurred. Just something ugly happening in the night. Something they cannot identify or pin down. Yet they know it has to do with death and fear and deadliness. No wonder they have called them the phantoms in the night. No wonder they cringe in their bowels."

"You say a peon is behind it. How about *Alcalde* Rodríguez? His blood isn't as blue as he claims, is it?

71

He'd love an upset that would help put him in the governor's seat."

Antonio made a disgusted sound. "That fop? It is impossible. It would take someone far more dangerous than he to build such an organization, to keep it so secret. My father must have known who it was. That is why he was killed."

"And now they think he passed the secret on to you. That's why they're after you."

The young man's face took on an even more ashen hue. All the affected hauteur and superciliousness were gone. Hayward saw the reason for it now, and pitied the boy. A kid, filled with fear, faced with the overwhelming responsibility of one of the biggest ranches in the country, trying to put on a show, trying to uphold the tradition of the haughty, unruffled *caballero,* afraid the whole thing would come to pieces if his people saw what was really inside him.

"Haven't you any idea who this leader is?" Hayward asked. "Not even a guess?"

The youth's eyes narrowed, and his face grew pinched. "Perhaps I have."

"Antonio," Carlota said, from the doorway.

Hayward wheeled to see her standing in the entrance to the hall. Her face was a satiny cameo in the gloom, big-eyed, full-lipped. She was in a black dress again, with its ribbed bodice pushing her breasts high. Hayward came to his feet.

"You have made enough of a spectacle of yourself," she told Antonio. "Please go to your room."

"Carlota, I. . . ."

"Antonio!"

Hayward saw a flush deepen in the man's face. He

72

moistened his lips, staring at his sister, and Hayward could almost feel the clash of their wills. Then Antonio dropped his eyes and walked to the door. She stepped aside to let him through. He looked up at her, seemed about to speak, then passed into the hall.

"You must forgive my brother," Carlota said. With a hiss of silk, she moved to the rosewood settee at the end of the room opposite the fireplace. Sitting down, she traced a finger across the striped tapestry upholstery, then raised her eyes to the baroque mirror above the settee. "We are indebted to your Yankee brigs for what small civilization we have out here. Not only the little luxuries, but the necessities . . . medicine and thread and needles and a million other things. The order closing our ports will reduce us to an unbearably primitive life once more. We are so cut off from the rest of the world. Some years ago the Manila galleon did not get through for several years. When it finally started coming again, it found even the most well-to-do of us dressed in rags."

She had watched him from the corner of her eye as she spoke, and he sensed that the monologue was intended to nullify what had happened between himself and Antonio.

"You're in sympathy with the Yankees, then?" he asked.

"My father was one of their staunchest supporters."

"*Alcalde* Rodríguez must love you."

She grinned. "Who cares for his opinion?"

"Do you think he was responsible for your father's death?"

Her eyes flashed angrily. She rose with that hiss of silk, walking to a sideboard. Her brother's quirt and gloves were there, and he had apparently knocked over one of the empty decanters with his drunken fumbling. She set it in place, saying thinly: "You must not listen to the maudlin ravings of Antonio. He is a man who would jump at his own shadow."

"Was it his shadow that shot him in the mountains?"

She wheeled on him. "How do we know it was the *fantasmas?* Has anybody ever seen them? Just a word . . . just a name before which the whole country cowers."

"I didn't say anything about the *fantasmas.*"

She flushed, her voice brittle. "You did."

Her angry breathing lifted her breasts against the top of her bodice. Her eyes were flashing fire. He had rarely seen a woman with so much spirit. It seemed to crackle through the room, touching off a corresponding excitement in him. It made him grin recklessly as he walked toward her.

"This must worry you as much as it does Antonio."

"It doesn't. It's too foolish!"

"Then why are you so excited?"

"I'm not excited . . . I'm not!"

He could see how he was goading her, and some perverse need to bring this haughty girl down off her pedestal kept him at it. "Yes, you are," he said. He stopped before her, grinning more broadly. "You're just as scared as Antonio. Why else would you be so jumpy?"

"Get out of here, before I call the servants."

"Why would you be so proud? Why would you ride around in that black coach with your nose turned up and lose your head and take the whip to anybody that mentioned the *fantasmas?*"

"I'm ordering you . . . get out!"

"Maybe I don't like to be ordered. Where I come from, a man doesn't jump through a hoop every time a pretty lady squeals at him."

With an inarticulate sound she snatched her brother's quirt from the sideboard and lashed him across the face

74

with it. Half blinded by the biting pain, he still managed to catch the quirt and tear it from her hand before she could strike again.

Then he grasped her by both shoulders and pinned her against the sideboard and kissed her. She struggled savagely, but he forced his weight against her, feeling the hot mold of her body to his, feeling the cushiony flattening of her breasts, digging his fingers into the satiny yielding of her back as he bent her over the sideboard. She moaned. Her whole body seemed to swell into his arms with a last spasmodic struggle, then she was completely quiescent against him. He stepped away, his own lips bruised from the savage pressure of the kiss.

"Now," he panted. "Want to whip me again?"

She didn't answer. There was pain still in her face, and rage. It dilated her pupils and made her cheeks flame. But there was passion, too, and a growing wonder. It made her lips full and pouting, and swelled her breasts with each shuddering breath till the ribbed top of her bodice dug deeply into the creamy flesh.

When she did not speak, he let a husky laugh flow from him, and turned and went out.

Chapter Seven

He couldn't help thinking about it, riding back to the corrals. A woman like Teresa, or Nita down at Callahan's, you could kiss and forget. But not Carlota. The kiss still remained with him, and he felt as if someone were stirring hot coals down inside his belly.

Well, that was natural. That's the kind of woman she was. Something special. That was all right, too. There had been other special ones. Marianne, in Santa Fé. Aveza, in Tripoli. And it hadn't caused him any trouble. It had just made the job that much more enjoyable. The whole trick was keeping it all in its proper relation to the job. And now he would do it with Carlota. She was something special, but he must keep it in relation.

Approaching the pens, he saw that Corado and a group of men were lined up at the bars of the big breaking corral, watching Pío Tico pitch around on the buckskin they had brought in from the mountains. Hayward saw that it was a real outlaw, full of dynamite and vinegar. The dust boiled up in yellow clouds, and the grunts of man and beast filled the pen.

Corado turned as Hayward rode up. "You look like the cat that got the cream," he said.

Hayward realized he must still be smiling to himself. "Good cream," he said, stepping down.

Corado saw the bloody cut across his face, and his eyes widened. "Don Antonio did that?" he asked.

"Carlota," Hayward said.

Corado's mouth dropped open. Then he threw back

76

his head and let out an explosive laugh. "Now we are truly *compadres*. We both got the same brand." The violent laugh diminished to a roguish chuckle. "You don't seem to mind it."

"After all," Hayward said, "how many men in this world get close enough to Carlota to get quirted by her?"

That started Corado laughing again and pounding him on the back. When he had finally subsided, he pulled Hayward over to the pen, a sweaty arm over his shoulder.

"You want to watch this. I think we have found one Pío Tico cannot bust, and it is driving him crazy."

The buckskin had stopped pitching around the corral and was trying to rear up. Pío Tico pounded his neck and spurred him cruelly, and the animal finally dropped to all fours and started to buck once more.

"Did you ever see such a magnificent one?" Corado asked. "Look at the balance. He changes leads so fast you cannot follow. What a roper he'll make! What a cutting horse! There he goes to rearing now. Tico will lose him again."

The horse reared high, pawing air. This time Pío Tico could not knock it down. It fell backward, and he had to drop off to keep from being crushed. The buckskin went clear over on its back, squealing and kicking. Then it rolled over and scrambled to its feet, snorting savagely. Pío Tico gained his feet and limped to the fence, his face dour and disgusted.

"That's a dozen times," Corado said angrily. "You might as well give up. If you can't break him of falling back, he won't be any good."

Hayward studied the buckskin. "They had a cure for that kind when I was in. . . ." He broke off. He had almost said *when I was in the Army*.

77

Corado glanced suspiciously at him. "When you were in where?"

"In Mexico," Hayward said.

"Why don't you show us?" Pío Tico said spitefully. "You're the big broncho buster. You're the sailor that can ride so good."

Hayward looked at the jealousy, the dislike in the man's face, realizing Pío Tico didn't think he could do it. He grinned and ducked through the poles, calling to the ropers for the horse. They caught it in a corner and held it blindfolded for him. Approaching, he saw how much horse it really was.

It only stood a little over fifteen hands, but its rump was massive, its chest overlaid with muscles that knotted and bunched like great fists as it shifted back and forth. It must have been fighting Pío Tico for half an hour, but it showed little sign of weariness. The smell of its sweat hung rancidly in the air, and its small grunting sounds were filled with unalloyed savagery. They had a hackamore on its snout, instead of a bridle, which was nothing new to Hayward, except that he had never seen so much rope used before. He tried to separate the different lines and find out what they did before he mounted. He discovered that only two of them controlled the horse, like a pair of reins, and the rest seemed to be there just for decoration or confusion. So he stepped aboard.

They tore the blind off, and the world exploded beneath him. He stuck with it till he saw the arched neck up against the sky and knew it was rearing with him. Instead of trying to spur it and knock the horse back down, he waited till the last instant, then dropped off.

He hit hard, rolled over like a cat, regaining his feet. He saw that the horse had fallen onto its back and was rolling over, too. He jumped for it, dodged a flailing hoof, and threw himself across its head.

The buckskin thrashed and squealed, but could gain no leverage. The weight of his body pinned its head, holding the animal down. The horse fought savagely, rolling and thrashing. But the leverage was against it. Finally, realizing it was helpless, the horse subsided. Hayward released it and got up. The buckskin rolled over, scrambled to its feet, snorting and whinnying in frustrated anger.

Hayward signaled to the ropers again, and they caught it. Once more he mounted. Once more it reared up. Once more he dropped off. And once more he held its head down while the horse fought savagely to get free. Finally it subsided in defeat, and he let it up.

He had to repeat the process half a dozen times. Each time it reared up, each time he held the animal's head while it fought him in a rage much more savage than anything it displayed on its feet. After it subsided in defeat that sixth time, he got to his feet, wobbly with exhaustion, covered with dust.

"Hayward," Corado shouted. "What the hell are you doing? We can't go on like this all day."

"You'll find out," Hayward said. "Can't you see how mad he is when I hold his head down? They hate that more than anything in the world."

The ropers had the buckskin again, and he dragged himself aboard. And this time it didn't rear. It started out bucking right away. He didn't think he'd ever had anything so savage between his legs. But it didn't rear.

He was too tired to stick long, and, when it went to sunfishing, he spilled hard. He rolled over and crawled to the fence while the riders hazed the buckskin to the other side of the pen. Corado ran down the fence and stooped

79

through, laughing raucously.

"What do you think of that, Tico? You ever see anything like it? Just sitting on his head. Why didn't we think of that? You got to be a clown, I guess."

Hayward was on his feet now, shaking his head, wiping the sweat-caked dust from his face. Pío Tico approached slowly, the jealousy apparent in his glittering eyes.

"How do we know he won't start it over again?" he asked.

"Because the habit's broken," Corado said. "You've seen enough horses to know that. One like this doesn't quit till he's really beat. He won't fall back again, and you know it."

A flush came to Pío Tico's narrow cheeks, and he spoke thinly to Hayward. "Why don't you go ahead and really bust him, then, if you're so good?"

"No," Corado said. "Not today. Maybe Hayward broke it of one bad habit, but there's still too much dynamite left in the horse. It would bust Hayward's guts. He's too tired for a ride like that. We'll wait till tomorrow."

El Sombrío called from the other end of the fence. "We got a dun over here that looks like it's got a Salazar brand on it. You want to check?"

Corado walked away from Hayward and Pío Tico, disappearing in the maze of pens and corrals. There was a studied insolence in the way Pío Tico kept his eyes on Hayward. He pulled a package of corn-shuck cigarette papers from his pocket, thumbed one free, and tapped the tobacco into it from a reed tube.

"You really must be his pet," he said, "the way he pampers you."

Hayward grinned. "And you don't like it."

A darker hue ran into Pío Tico's face. He got out his

80

steel *eslabón,* his red cord of tinder, his flint. He struck a spark on the flint with the *eslabón,* lodged it in the tinder, and blew it into flame.

"I guess you couldn't ride it anyway," he said, lighting his cigarette. "I guess Corado knows that." He blew the tinder out, put his makings back into a buckskin sack, and deposited it in his pocket. "You just got a little trick . . . makes it look like you're a real broncho buster."

Hayward knew what the man was doing, but he couldn't help feeling goaded. He felt the other men watching him — Gregorio, Pablo, Nicolás. He knew that in their eyes he had been issued a sort of challenge, and would lose stature if he backed down. And he suddenly realized he could not afford to lose that stature. One of the greatest possibilities of finding Bardine was through these people. And the surest way to lose any confidence he had gained was by a show of weakness. He grinned.

"Throw the ropes on again," he said. "I'll show you another little trick."

They cornered the horse and roped him and blindfolded him once more. Walking toward the buckskin, Hayward knew this was going to be different. He was tired, and the horse would really blow its cork. But it was something he had to do, if he wanted to stand as a man among these people.

He stepped up, settling himself in the high-cantled saddle. He nodded, and they pulled the blind off, the ropes. A thousand pounds of buckskin fury erupted between Hayward's legs.

The horse bogged his head and started bucking straightaway. Hayward had never been an official broncho buster when he was handling the horses for Leavenworth, but he'd topped enough green ones to know the business.

81

He rode with a slack body, taking each jar like a wet dish rag, calculating the switches before they came.

The horse came out of the straight pitching and shifted to a left lead, and Hayward sensed a sunfisher coming. He was already shifting his weight to the left as the horse threw its right shoulder down. It twisted so far its belly flashed in the sun like a great trout breaking water. As it came up and changed leads again, Hayward was already throwing his weight the other way. The left shoulder went down, the left side rolled up. But Hayward was twisted over onto the opposite side, changing his weight to catch the horse coming back up.

The buckskin straightened out, squealing in anger as it realized Hayward was still there. It sunfished again, even more violently. Without thought, Hayward shifted his weight, back and forth, hanging on with all he had.

As he came out of it the second time, he had a glimpse of Corado, running back toward the corral. Then the horse had reached the end of the pen. Hayward thought it would spin around, and so started shifting his center of balance. But the animal waited an instant longer than he had expected. It almost tore him out of the saddle when the spin finally came. Barely hanging on, he saw the fence coming at him, and realized what was happening.

He jerked his right leg free of the stirrup and kicked high with it. The buckskin's rump smashed into the fence so hard the whole pen shuddered. If Hayward's foot had been in the stirrup, his leg would have been smashed.

"Hayward!" Corado shouted. "Take a spill! You can't ride that crazy fool out. He's going for it again!"

The horse spun back, charged the fence once more. Hayward waited till the last instant for the spin and this time kicked his left leg free. The horse spun against the fence with a shuddering smash once more. And once more Hayward's leg would have caught between fence and horse if he hadn't kicked free.

Screaming in rage, the buckskin wheeled away. Hayward sought the stirrups once more. The horse started pitching in circles and figure eights all over the corral. Hayward had a jarring vision of the corral spinning around him, the shouting men, the blue sky, the tawny earth. He knew he was tiring. He kept losing contact, didn't know which way he was headed. When a man lost that much control, he was on the way to getting his brains spilled all over the corral. It was time to dive.

But maybe Pío Tico's insolence had made him mad. Or maybe it was the horse beneath him, so much wilder and more savage than anything he'd ever topped before that it filled him with a matching desire, just as wild and savage, to conquer it. Or maybe he'd been slammed around so much now he couldn't think straight.

"Look out, Hayward, he's going to try to wipe you off again!"

Hayward would not have felt the change of leads but for Corado's shout. His dulled senses responded to the voice more than to the shifting horse beneath him. He altered his balance, getting ready to kick free on the left side. The spin came. He lashed his foot out of the stirrup and kicked high. The buckskin's rump slammed into the fence with a deafening crash of wood. The horse spun away with an enraged scream, trying on the other side.

"Hayward!"

Again he was almost too late, again it was the voice that jarred him over onto the side, making him tear his leg free. The horse screamed once more as it spun away and realized Hayward was still sticking. It started pioneering, never

83

coming down in the same place twice. Hayward went crazy trying to follow its wild gyrations with his shifting weight.

Even with the agonized effort of staying on, Hayward could not help marveling at the incredible balance of the animal. It was always perfectly collected in its wildest attempts to unseat him. It never got off balance, shifting leads with amazing instinct, never unsupported in a spin or a landing.

After the pioneering, it pitched straightaway, heading for the fence again. Hayward saw the bars coming at him, heard Corado shout again.

"Hayward, take a dive! He'll wipe you off for sure this time. You're getting fuzzy. Take a dive!"

But the buckskin spun before reaching the fence. With a savage triumph, Hayward knew the horse had given up that trick just as it had given up falling backward when it realized that had failed.

But the beast began pile driving now. In a last frenzy of rage, it reached for the clouds, coming down with all four feet planted. The whole world seemed to explode in Hayward's head. The dust billowed about him like a yellow fog. He was choking on it, and blood was streaming from his ears and nostrils. All he had left was his grim resolve to stay on.

Again and again his body jerked to that hammering blow against the end of his spine. Again and again he heard the earth shudder and the horse scream. He didn't know how much longer it lasted. He came out of the mad nightmare to find himself belly down over the big saddle horn. The horse was no longer erupting beneath him. It was standing with four legs braced, head down, dirty lather unfurling from it in great dripping ropes. Its whole great body was shaking, and the breath was passing through it with a painful, wheezing sound.

Corado and the others came running out to lift him down. Corado tore his own bandanna off and wiped Hayward's face, laughing and shouting, and then sopped the blood from his nose.

"¡Madre de Dios!" Corado yelled. "Did you see that ride? I haven't watched anything like it, not in twenty years. Did you see it, Sombrío?" He pounded Hayward on the back. "You bastard! I thought you'd be killed for sure. What a jinete you'll make! I thought he'd wipe you off that fence a dozen times. Jinete, hell. ¡Amansador! That's what you'll be, you son-of-a-bitch, the best god-damn amansador California ever. . . ."

He broke off suddenly, as if a new thought had come to his mind. The childish enthusiasm was swept from him. He turned to glare at Pío Tico, his face contorted, the diffused blood sweeping into his cheeks till they looked almost black. Without warning, he swung his arm out in a backhand blow that caught Pío Tico full in the face, knocking him head over heels across the corral.

"That's for giving Juanito a devil like that to ride," he shouted. Then he whirled around and slammed Hayward with another backhand blow. It knocked Hayward through the men and spilled him heavily onto his back. "And that's for disobeying my orders," he said. "What the hell am I, your wet nurse or something, that I must follow you around and keep your diapers clean?"

Chapter Eight

The first heat of summer came to Rancho del Sur on the morning after Hayward broke the buckskin. He was stiff and sore from the beating he had taken on the horse, and was content to sit against the wall of El Sombrío's hovel, soaking up the sun. Drowsily he watched the men gathering at the corrals, listened to the cries of the half-naked children at play, and let his eyes wander across the broad meadows to the haze-silvered backdrop of timber beyond. A feeling slowly came to him that a man could very happily remain in this indolent, golden land for the rest of his life.

El Sombrío came out and sat down against the wall, fingering his *penitente* flute. "The fog was pink this morning. It means the sun will burn the grass out this summer and leave us no forage for next year."

Eyes closed, Hayward chuckled. "You don't fool me, you old scoundrel. You know there isn't any such thing as a bad omen in this country. You never spent a bad day in all your life, and you're just afraid somebody will find out how easy you've had it and take it away from you."

El Sombrío dug him slyly with an elbow. "You have discovered my secret, Juanito. It is true. Nobody can be unhappy in this land. And now I will tell you your secret. When you first came here, it was just another place to you. That grin, that laugh, they only covered a great restlessness. You were just waiting for the time you could leave."

Hayward was surprised. "I guess you're right. Seems like I've been traveling most of my life. One spot seemed

86

like the next. Always looking for the greener pasture, the prettier girl."

"Until now," El Sombrío said. "I've seen it before, about this country. It casts a spell over a man. It is getting under your skin and soon you will not be able to leave." His face saddened. "Once that was good. Once it was a golden land, with nothing but this peace, this laughing, this sleeping in the sun. Now, beneath all those things, there is something frightening."

"What if we got rid of that? Wouldn't we find the peace again?"

El Sombrío made a rough sound. "I told you I would not talk of that again. You have enough to worry about, right here."

"Looks peaceful enough to me."

"It is Pío Tico," El Sombrío said. "Have you not noticed his jealousy? Before you came, Corado was teaching Tico all he knew, was going to make an *amansador* of him. But now Corado sees how much better you are than Tico, and we all know what is in his mind. He is going to make you the *protegido*, and Tico will be cast aside."

"That's bad?"

"To understand how bad, you must understand fully what *amansador* means to us. It is much more than just the foreman of the ranch, who oversees the gathering of the cattle, the catching of the horses, their breaking and gentling and training. An *amansador* here occupies a position of respect, of reverence, which has little parallel in your land. For this is a country of horsemen, Juanito, and the *amansador* is the king of all horsemen. He does not usually reach such a position till late in life. It is the result of a lifetime of training, of learning, of labor. He starts in childhood, goes through years of riding the rough string as

87

a *jinete,* more long years under the tutelage of some famous *amansador.* Only after a painful apprenticeship of half a lifetime is a man worthy of being called an *amansador.* He then has the infinite knowledge of men and horses that entitles him to the name."

"Corado is pretty young for it, then, isn't he?"

"That's why he is so rare," El Sombrío said. "You can understand how all the young *jinetes* hope and pray for the day any *amansador* will take one of them under his wing. It is like a religious rite to them. Even with an ordinary *amansador* there is fierce competition among the young men to be the chosen one. But in a land where the *amansador* is king, Miguel Corado is king of the *amansadores.* He is envied and emulated and worshipped not only by the *jinetes,* but by all other *amansadores* as well. Now, can you appreciate what it meant to Tico to have you take his place with Corado?"

It was like a revelation to Hayward. He had seen enough glimpses of the worship, the awe, the love with which all the people regarded Corado. Now, however, it was as if he understood those feelings fully for the first time, and their reasons. El Sombrío saw the understanding in his face, and nodded solemnly.

"I think you can see it now. And I think you know what a dangerous thing has started. Tico would do almost anything to get back in the favor of Corado."

Hayward did not answer. He was remembering the glittering jealousy in Pío Tico's eyes the day before. It was still lying darkly in his mind as he saw Nieves emerge from the grove of cottonwoods that grew along the stream at the end of the lane. She had risen early to do the washing and carried a basket piled high with snowy linens and cottons. With her was another woman. As they drew closer, Hayward saw that it was Aline Bardine.

"Look who came to visit us, Sombrío," Nieves said. "She is going to help me with the wash."

El Sombrío winked slyly. "You cannot fool me. She came to see Corado."

"Well, she will still help me with the wash," Nieves said.

There was a healthy peasant glow to Aline's buxom beauty. Her pleated blouse fell off one sleek, gleaming shoulder, and the ripeness of heavily fleshed thighs curved against a sleazy calico skirt. It was a different kind of beauty than Carlota's, a vivid, robust vitality that reached out to Hayward and kindled the animal things deep down inside him.

He came to his feet, grinning at her. She stopped by the door, holding his eyes solemnly, not answering the smile. El Sombrío got to his feet, glancing shrewdly at them.

"I got business at the horse corral," he said. "You leave this one alone, Juanito. She belongs to Corado."

He shambled off, fingering his flute. Nieves called Aline, and the girl went inside. She reappeared carrying a big basket of dirty clothes. Hayward offered to help her with it, and they carried it between them toward the grove of poplars.

"What did you find in the mountains?" she asked. "Tico said there was some kind of trouble."

"Somebody took a shot at Antonio Mateo up there," he said.

"The *fantasmas?*"

"Antonio thought so."

He kept looking at her. There weren't many so ripe. She made him forget Carlota for the moment. It was truly a golden land.

They were within the grove now, with the dappled

89

shadows falling across the gleaming curve of her bare shoulder. She set the basket down and came around it to stand before him. She looked up at him with that solemn naïveté in her eyes, like a little child.

"Won't you tell me why you are really here?" she asked.

"I'm a sailor," he said. "I'm serving out a sentence."

She clutched at his arm, her underlip quivering. "Don't torture me like this. If you are really a spy, if you are after my father, tell me."

"I wish I could," he said.

"You can." Her voice broke. "I need it so badly, Juanito. I've waited so long, hoping for some word of Father. He's the only one I have in the world. If I only knew someone had been sent in to find him."

There was a painful need in her shining young face, and he wanted to help her, wanted to give her the reassurance his true identity would hold, as one would want to help a child. But suspicion born of too many past betrayals held him back.

"Look," he said. "I can't tell you a lie just to make you feel good. But maybe this will help. I guess Pío Tico told you what we found in the Santa Lucias. That trapper, James Morgan. . . ."

"I don't know anything about him," she said.

"What?"

Her eyes fluttered. "That is, the name doesn't mean anything. Tico asked me about it this morning."

He frowned at her. "There were others in that building with Morgan. They got away. In the fight, I pulled off somebody's button. It looked as if it came from some kind of military coat."

He fished it from his pocket. She stared at it. Her cheeks turned pale. She took it from his hand, along with

90

the bit of blue cloth clinging to it.

"My father," she said breathlessly. "He was a captain in the Navy. He still had his coat. The buttons had anchors on them, just like this."

It struck Hayward like a blow. Had he been that close to the man? A sense of defeat, of frustration, of useless loss ran through him like nausea. He tried to cover the reaction.

"Was he wearing the coat the night they took him?"

Her eyes were squinted shut, the tears squeezing from them. She nodded her head mutely. Then she caught his arms, her fingers digging in.

"Hayward, you've got to tell me now. You have come to save him, haven't you? There's no use hiding it any longer." All the lushness of her young body was forcing its cushiony curves against him. "You know now that they're holding him out there somewhere. He's not dead. There's a chance of saving him. Please tell me. You were so close, and now you're going back out. Tell me you're going to try again. Please, please tell me we've got help!"

That need was naked in her face now. She was clinging to him like a child. Her eyes were shining with tears, and her lips were parted. Automatically his arms went around her waist, his fingers spread against the satiny flesh of her back, just above the swelling curve of her backside. It was a powerful plea. He knew he couldn't stand against it any longer, knew he had to tell her.

"Aline," he said. "I. . . ."

The jingle of spurs cut him off. He turned to see Corado standing within the trees, looking as surprised as they did. Flushing with embarrassment, Aline pulled away. Corado was just finishing a tamale, and he stuffed the last enormous segment in his mouth, unconcernedly letting the rich brown juice dribble down his chin.

91

"Don't stop," he said, with a full mouth. "I didn't mean to interrupt."

Aline bent to gather up the spilled clothes and pile them in a basket. "You didn't interrupt anything," she said. "I was just going."

She sent Hayward a strange, wide-eyed look, then wheeled with the basket under one arm and hurried on through the trees toward the creek. Corado followed the jiggle of her backside with a lecherous leer.

"My admiration for you is growing daily," he told Hayward. "Not only do you tame the roughest mustang we have had in years, but you got the ripest plum on the ranch hot as a tamale for you."

"You aren't angry?"

"Why should I be angry?"

"I thought she was your girl."

Corado threw back his head to let out a roaring laugh. "My friend, my friend! When will you understand Miguel Corado? There are a million girls. Last night Aline was my girl. Tomorrow Nita will be my girl. Who cares? If Aline does not suit you, just come to me. I know a dozen more down in Monterey you can have."

Hayward had to join in the gusty laughter.

Corado throttled down to a chuckle, belching comfortably, patting his stomach. "Now," he said. "You feel good enough to make love, you should feel good enough to work the buckskin. He's busted for good. His training has got to start. If an *amansador* you are going to be, there is no time to waste."

Hayward hesitated, remembering what El Sombrío had said. It was true, then. Hayward had taken Pío Tico's place. But that was not what made him hesitate. His whole impulse now was not to waste any more time, to get away somehow, to start the search for Bardine. Yet he knew how foolish that impulse was. If they had been holding Bardine in Higuera Cañon that night, they would not return. They would take him to a new spot, and that might be any place within a thousand miles. Hayward would be a fool to lose what he had gained here by making a break for it just to go on a wild-goose chase like that.

It was a bitter pill to take, but it was something he had learned through long apprenticeship. Patience. In the long run, that was the only weapon he had in his search. The patience to sit it out, to wait for the breaks, to become close enough to these people to win their confidence and find out their secrets. He had broken the horse yesterday to win their confidence. Corado's offer now proved how successful he had been. And now he would have to go on with it, no matter what a waste of time it seemed.

He grinned suddenly. "Let's go," he said.

The buckskin was alone in a big pen, trotting restlessly up and down the fence. It still had that look of smoldering, latent explosion, with the muscles bunching like fists in its chest, rippling like fat snakes across the heavy rump. The action was high and square, and it turned like a bull, with a sudden fiddle of front hoofs and a quick flip of its rump.

It was not a beautiful horse in the classical sense. But it emanated a sense of fire and spirit and primitive savagery that made its every motion, its every pose reach out and capture fascinated attention from a man. The two of them watched it for a long time in the silent communion of horse lovers. Finally Corado stirred reluctantly.

"Callahan . . . he tells me the way a lot of you Americans break a horse is to put the bit in the mouth from the first," he said. "A *californio* would rather die than do that. You cut the poor colt's mouth to pieces, pulling and hauling and jerking on him, when he doesn't even know the signals yet. If you do not ruin him, you end up with an iron-mouthed horse that reins like an elephant.

"You must have felt how collected he was when you rode him. Never lost his balance, never a wrong lead. Gentle him and train and polish him right, and he'll make the best cutting horse Rancho del Sur ever had. You took the bucking out of him, and he's broke now, and that makes him ready to be turned over to the *amansador*. Instead of taking him myself, I'm going to let you have him. I'll show you how to put him through every stage of training. He's marvelous material. How he turns out depends on what kind of an *amansador* you make. Let's begin, eh?"

Corado got a reata off the top rail and forefooted the buckskin. Then, while Hayward saddled him up, Corado got the *jaquima de domar*.

"This is the starting hackamore," he told Hayward. "It's what you had on him the other day. I know you're used to riding a bitted horse when you're busting it. You're just liable to tear the poor *potro*'s mouth to pieces, and, if he had the makings of a good cow horse, you've ruined him right there. A colt's mouth and bars aren't mature enough when he's this age. You ever see a *jaquima de domar* before like this? This horsehair rope we use for the reins is called the *mecate*. It takes place of the bit. You see how the *mecate* is attached to the bosal. You don't have to pull hard on the *mecate* to cut off his wind. That's the control. We'll just do a bit of starting and stopping this afternoon, eh?"

"You going to leave this lead rope on?" asked Hayward.

"That is the *fiador*," said Corado. "You'll see how it works."

"Looks like you've got enough rope for a dozen hangings."

Corado grinned. "They're twenty-two feet long. It seems like a lot of line at first, but it has its uses. The rawhide part is the noseband. The big knot is tied in the tender spot just beneath the jaw. You pull on the reins, and the knot digs in. That horse'll learn what you want pretty quick. And you aren't even touching his mouth."

Hayward had worked with some forms of the hackamore before, but had never seen such a complex arrangement. He saw why the *mecate* was so long, now. After looping one end around the horse's neck for reins, Corado left about twelve feet dangling from the knot beneath the jaw, to use as a lead rope. Hayward stepped up. The horse stood bunched and quivering beneath Hayward, but did not start bucking. With a triumphant chuckle, Corado took the lead rope in his hands.

"Give him the heels," he said.

Hayward gathered up the long horsehair reins, touched the buckskin with his heels. The horse snorted, fiddled, but did not go forward. Corado nodded. Hayward used his heels again. At the same time, Corado tugged on the lead rope. It dug the knot into the tender spot beneath the buckskin's jaw. The horse jumped, responding to the pull, lurching forward. They repeated the process a dozen times, moving around the corral, Corado pulling on the rope every time Hayward heeled the buckskin. Then Corado dropped the lead rope and stepped back, telling Hayward to use the heels alone. The horse responded without the added pull on the rope, starting forward promptly.

"What did I tell you?" Corado crowed. "We've got the smartest horse in California here. Some jugheads . . . they take a month before they'll answer the heels without a drag on the rope. Now stop him, Juanito."

Hayward gave a slight pull on the horsehair reins. The

horse's head snapped up, and it came to a sharp halt, fiddling back and forth.

"Too heavy on the reins," shouted Corado. "Keep pulling him that way and you'll have a head tosser. *¡Válgame Dios!* You must have mutton chops for hands. You aren't fit to rein a blind mule."

Hayward flushed under the rebuke. He had always been considered a light-handed rider. He slacked up, and the horse settled down. Then Corado told him to use the heels again, and he put the horse into motion. Hayward used a lighter pull to stop the buckskin, and the animal came to a halt without jerking its head. They spent the rest of the afternoon that way, and Hayward soon realized what an exacting teacher he had. His slightest mistake elicited a storm of rebuke, and more than once he thought Corado was going to pull him bodily off the horse.

"No, no, get those reins away from his neck. You aren't ready to start turning him. Do I have to get up there and show you myself? You're giving him more bad habits in a day than Tico could pick up in a lifetime. Why did I ever pick such a stupid fool . . . ?"

That was how the days passed. Hayward had thought he was a finished horseman, but he felt like a beginner in the face of these strange new methods. There seemed a million things to learn. How to make the *falsarienda* by taking wraps in the hackamore; why horsehair from the mane was the best for the reins; how to attach the sliding brow band so it could be used as a blind for mounting a spooky horse. He worked endlessly on the sliding stop, on teaching the animal to back straight and fast, and on the jump-off and the turns and the spins. But despite the fascination of watching such a magnificent animal develop, Bardine was always at the back of his mind.

96

He was constantly on the lookout for some excuse to get away without arousing suspicion, some way to renew the search again. He knew early roundup was coming and hoped it might give him a chance to get into the mountains again. But his chance was to come sooner than that.

Two weeks after Hayward had first broken the buckskin, Antonio and his retinue of riders and retainers went to Monterey to settle with Colonel Archuleta about the consignment of beef for the troops. The next noon, Hayward and Corado were working the buckskin in the corral when a lone horseman appeared on the Monterey road. As he neared, Corado said he was Valentino Castillo, one of the rich young landholders along the Salinas, a drinking companion of Antonio's. He was typical of his class — slim, dark, elegantly dressed, graceful in the saddle. He drew his lathered animal to a halt by the corrals. His hands fluttered nervously on the reins, and there was a sense of strain beneath the dust-filmed surface of his narrow face.

"Has Don Antonio come home yet?"

"No, *señor*. He is still down in Monterey."

Castillo fiddled with his reins. "That's just it. He isn't."

Corado moved closer to him. "What?"

The man sighed heavily, clamped his lips together, then said: "Do you know of the Gilroy brothers, up on the Carmel River?"

"The Americans who refused to grind any more flour for Monterey till Rodríguez opens the port again?"

"The same ones," Castillo said. "It all started over that. It is working a great hardship on everyone, since there is no other mill in the country, and there is much feeling. Last night half a dozen of us were at the Pacific House. We all got very drunk, and Gallegos suggested we go up and force the Gilroys to start grinding again. In our state,

97

it sounded like a gay escapade. The Gilroys were not home when we arrived, and we broke in and found more wine. Then, drunker still, we separated to look for the Americans. Gallegos went with Antonio to the mill, which is a half mile upriver from the house. It was not yet dawn, and somehow, in the darkness, Gallegos lost Antonio. We thought he would return and waited. But Antonio did not show up. We hunted through the mountains for him but could find no sign. We thought perhaps he had returned here."

Corado shook his head. "He has not returned. I am sure of it. You better go tell the *Señorita* Carlota. I will get some men and saddle up."

Chapter Nine

Corado would not let Hayward use the buckskin, saying it was not yet ready for such a trip, so Hayward roped out a roan and a couple of spares, throwing his saddle on the roan. By the time Pío Tico and El Sombrío had joined them, there was a commotion up by the big house. Hayward saw a procession leave the door and proceed toward the corrals — a half dozen cotton-clad servants, Valentino Castillo, Carlota's Aunt Adela, and Carlota herself. It seemed a repetition of what Hayward had seen before, with the fat, black-clad aunt wringing her hands and pleading with Carlota.

"Please, little one, the country will be scandalized. No woman of your station can go on such a ride . . . and such a shocking costume! You will be ostracized. You will be ruined."

Carlota came grimly toward the corral, paying no attention. She had piled her hair into the crown of a flat-topped hat. She wore a rawhide jacket over a white silk blouse, pulled in tight at the waist by a broad red sash. She had put on a pair of her brother's rawhide breeches, split to the knee to reveal the white linen beneath. They had been cut for much narrower hips than she possessed, and clung like wet paint to her round curves. Hayward saw Corado take in all that. There was none of the obvious lechery he took such a delight in revealing with other women. His eyes, for just a moment, looked like glowing coals in his dark face.

She stopped before him, slapping her quirt into the

palm of her hand. "Now," she said. "We are not going through this again, are we?"

Corado said: "I must protest."

"Very well. You have registered your protest, and my aunt has registered her protest. I am still going."

They tried to talk her out of it. But she was adamant, and finally they had to saddle a horse for her. Castillo was plainly scandalized and thrilled by such a flouting of tradition, and followed the whole procedure with awed eyes. They left the ranch with Aunt Adela still pleading and crying, and headed straight across the broad meadows into the mountains.

Carlota had not spoken to Hayward, but now he caught her glance on him. He looked squarely at her, grinning broadly. Her lips compressed, and she looked away. He had seen little of her since the day of that kiss, but he was glad to believe it was still on her mind.

It took them the better part of the day to reach the headwaters of the Carmel, fighting their way through the steep and jagged Santa Lucias on little-used trails. They followed the river down through redwood-studded forests, attained a trail that paralleled the water for a while, then wound over a bluff and down onto alfalfa-covered flats. Here was the Gilroy house, dour, sun-bleached adobe with thatched roof and oilskin windowpanes. There was no stock in the corrals. The door was gaping open. It was ominously quiet.

Carlota and most of the men dismounted and trooped inside. The room was barren and dirt-floored, with a few pieces of meager furniture. There were some broken jugs on the floor, and the table had been overturned. Castillo ruefully admitted the drunken young men had done that the night before. After he spoke, the silence fell again, with

100

only the scrape of their boots against the floor, the huskiness of their breathing. Carlota looked at Corado.

"Isn't it strange?"

The man shrugged. "What's the difference? We could find out nothing from the Gilroys. They were not even here when Don Antonio disappeared."

"But he knew them," she said. "He might have met with them. They handle their stock about a mile down the river, where there is more open ground. Perhaps they went on roundup early this year and are branding down there. Or they might be at the mill. We should find them before we go on, Corado. There is something funny here."

He sighed heavily. "Very well. We will go to their pens. Hayward, you and Sombrío go up to the mill. Meet us here in half an hour."

Hayward and the old man followed the broad and shallow river up toward the bluff. It narrowed here, and began to reveal shelving drop-offs that provided natural formations for a dam and millpond. The creaking of the wheel was audible now, a forlorn sound in the surrounding silence. They rounded the bluff and saw the mill, a tall, hip-roofed structure of shaggy redwood logs. They neared the open door and dismounted, peering inside.

The clank of the wheel's machinery was so loud they did not hear the other sound at first. Then Hayward caught it, and moved into the shadowy door. The first large chamber was filled with sacks of grain piled almost to the ceiling. The stench of rotting wheat almost gagged Hayward. It was so dark here he could hardly see, and he bumped into a heavy upright. El Sombrío caught his arm apprehensively.

"I do not like this. There is something strange."

"Take it easy," Hayward said. "What's that noise?"

They moved down the lane between the piled sacks,

101

reached a stairway leading to an upper level. Hayward identified the sound as voices, now, apparently two men arguing in the upper room. He began to climb the stairs, and the words became recognizable above the grind and clank of machinery. With a start of surprise, Hayward realized it was Rodríguez's spiteful, lisping voice.

"I will have none of your insolence. I came up here to settle this. I want that flour shipped to Monterey. I want you to start grinding again."

Hayward's head was above the upper level then, and he could make out the two men in the other room, standing beside the huge, grating grindstone. Rodríguez made an elephantine shape in the gloom, black satin cloak hanging clear to the tops of his wing boots. The other man was apparently one of the Gilroy brothers. A lifetime of grueling labor had molded him. He was big and ponderous as a Percheron, the muscles bunched and knotted across his upper back and shoulders. His pale red hair had been bleached by the sun till it glowed like a nimbus in the dusky room, and the shape of his heavy-boned face was square and stubborn. They had apparently been arguing for some time, because they were both tense and ruddy with anger. Gilroy's voice came in a rough gust.

"You know you didn't have no right to close that port to the Americans. Governor Pico didn't authorize it . . . Mexico City's hopping mad about it . . . half your own people here don't want it. I'll grind your flour again when you let the Yankee brigs in again."

"I make no compromises, *Señor* Dan," Rodríguez sputtered. His jowls were red as turkey wattles. "If you don't obey my orders, I will send the troops up here."

"Why didn't you do that in the first place? Colonel Archuleta wouldn't back you up, would he? You couldn't

102

get him up here, so you have to come yourself."

With a curse, Rodríguez grabbed the man's shirt, shouting in his face. "I said I wanted no insolence!"

"Take your hands off me!"

"Don't tell me what to do, you Yankee pig!"

Dan Gilroy shifted his weight and brought a short, vicious blow into the man's paunch. With a surprising swiftness, Rodríguez spun away from the blow, and it missed him completely. Before Gilroy could recover, the *alcaldes* tepped back in and smashed him across the face. It was a brutal, chopping blow, by a man who knew what he was doing. It knocked Gilroy backward to fall heavily against a sack of grain. He rolled over and came to his knees, face slack with the shock of the blow. Before he could come to his feet, Rodríguez followed him and kicked him in the belly.

Hayward saw the boot sink deeply, saw Gilroy spill aside, and jackknife with pain. It was automatic for Hayward to jump up the steps and into the room to keep the fight from going further. Rodríguez wheeled, his mouth gaping in surprise — but not so much surprise to be unable to reach beneath his cloak. Hayward saw the brass mounting of a pistol flash dully in the dim light.

"It would be a dear price to pay," Rodríguez said.

Hayward stopped, staring down the muzzle of the gun, letting a husky breath flow from him. El Sombrío was directly behind him, checked by the gun, too. Gilroy dragged himself to a sitting position against the sack of grain, hugging his belly. His face looked jaundiced with nausea. It gave Hayward a new estimation of Rodríguez.

"Quite a different rôle for you," he said.

"Perhaps too many people think me a fop," Rodríguez said peevishly.

103

"Perhaps it pleases you to have them do so."

The *alcalde*'s pouched eyes grew slitted. "Are you going to be insolent, as well? What are you doing here, sailor?"

"We came looking for Antonio Mateo."

"I, too, am on that mission. I heard he was last seen here. Something mysterious is going on here."

"Perhaps the *fantasmas?*"

A little muscle fluttered through the *alcalde*'s cheek. He bent forward, squinting to see Hayward better in the dim light. "What do you know of them?"

"Not much. Except that you think they're a bunch of Yankees."

Rodríguez threw his arm out in an angry, theatrical gesture. "What else could they be? A bunch of Yankees wanting to overthrow me here, led by a Yankee."

"Named James Morgan?"

Again Rodríguez bent forward sharply, blinking at Hayward. His voice sounded strained. "What do you know of him?"

"What do *you* know of him?"

"Now you are being insolent again. For all I know, you are a *fantasma*, too. I should have you thrown back in jail. I should have you hung on the highest tree." He broke off with a sudden bleat, as Gilroy stirred behind him. He whirled toward the man, jerking his pistol around. Then he called shrilly: "Ugardes! Where are you, Ugardes?"

"Right here, *señor*," the man said.

The voice came from behind Hayward, a soft purr that made him wheel sharply. Ugardes stood at the foot of the stairs in the lower room. His face was a pale wedge in the gloom; his eyes looked green as a cat's. For a moment there was no sound save the groan of the giant shaft, the clatter of cogs, the grating of the huge grindstone. Then

104

Ugardes said: "I could not find the other Gilroy by the dam. I thought perhaps you might need me."

"It's about time," Rodríguez said breathlessly. "These *bribónes* were ready to attack me. I was all alone, and they. . . ."

"I was here all the time, *señor.*"

"Eh?" The *alcalde* blinked his eyes. "You were?" He cleared his throat grumpily. "Well, why didn't you let me know?"

"You were in no danger."

"Of course, I wasn't." Rodríguez's foppishness was returning. He pouted his swinish lips and thrust out his paunch, flourishing the pistol at Gilroy. "And you will have that flour in Monterey by tomorrow . . . or else!"

He waved Hayward aside with the gun and stamped past, shaking the stairway with his waddling weight as he descended to the lower level. Ugardes let him pass, smiled enigmatically at Hayward, then followed the *alcalde* out.

Hayward walked to Gilroy. "Any permanent damage?"

The man got to his feet, grimacing sickly. "I guess not. He must be like a bull. I never met a man that could knock me down."

"I think a lot of people underestimate the good *alcalde*," Hayward said. Then he asked: "How about Antonio? Where were you last night?"

Gilroy looked angrily at El Sombrío, then said: "We saw that bunch of young drunks coming down the road. We figured they meant to make us start grinding again. We knew we couldn't stand against so many. We high-tailed it to the hills, stock and all. I just come back about half an hour ago to check the damage here, and Rodríguez popped out of nowhere."

"Was he really interested in Antonio?"

105

"Didn't even ask me about him."

"I thought it was strange he'd be so far from Monterey without any more escort than Ugardes," Hayward said.

"The *alcalde*'s a strange man," Gilroy remarked. Then he shook his head. "Far as Antonio's concerned, my brother and me run into a bunch of Indians near the coast last night. Sign language, mostly. Got the idea they was talking about a crazy man that rode into their camp around midnight, fell off his horse, then started shooting at them and yelling and everything when they tried to help him. Finally run off into the timber, I guess. That might've been Antonio."

Hayward told Corado and Carlota of that when they met once more at the house. Gilroy had said the Indian camp was about five miles down the coast in one of the steep ravines that opened out onto the beach. It took them the rest of the afternoon to find the ravine.

Backed up against the steep slope were the huts, mere cones of mud and reeds with a door a man had to crawl through. A cook fire smoked before one, surrounded by a group of Indians, squatting on the ground. Two of them rose as the riders approached; the others remained crouched indifferently on their haunches.

Hayward had seen many Indian tribes in Mexico, and thought he had seen the lowest on the scale. But none could compare with the degradation of these people. Most of them were completely naked, caked with dirt and filth, their eyes red-rimmed and heavy-lidded with the indifference of chronic disease and malnutrition. Their hair was thick as brush, growing low on their simian foreheads, and their hands were so dirty and so thickly callused they looked like horny claws.

Carlota glanced at Corado, and, when he did not speak,

106

she asked: "They are Mutsunes, are they not?"

He sent her a sullen look from beneath his heavy black brows, before finally turning to speak with one of the Indians. Hayward had to strain to make out any definite words.

"He will not answer my questions directly," Corado said in Spanish. "He invites us to eat."

"Would it make them any more friendly if we did?" Carlota asked.

"I don't know. I don't think you would like to eat with them, anyway."

Carlota glanced at what the people were fingering from a stew pot. "What is it?"

"A paste made from dried grasshoppers."

Carlota's lips grew thin. "I'm afraid," she said, "that we will have to get what information we can without accepting their invitation to eat."

Corado watched her a moment, enigmatically, then turned back to question the Indian again. Hayward stared around the indescribably primitive camp, similar to the dens of wild beasts, realizing that these were Corado's origins. It allowed Hayward to understand more fully the man's primitive violence, his childish transition of moods, his cruelties, and his lusts.

Finally the man turned to Carlota again and said: "I can get nothing out of them."

Pío Tico glanced sharply at Corado, then dropped his eyes. Carlota caught the look and frowned suspiciously at Pío Tico.

"Is that true?" she said. "Your mother was an Indian."

"A Tirus, *señorita*, from Yerba Buena."

"The language isn't that much different, Tico. Why did you look like that?" she asked. He glanced guiltily at Corado and dropped his eyes before the man's glare.

107

Carlota whirled to Corado. Her voice was rising. "Don't try to spare me. If Antonio passed this way, and there was trouble, I must know." She danced her horse against the black, grasping Corado's arm. "Don't try to spare me, Corado. I will find out, anyway. I will order Tico to talk with them."

Hayward saw a deep flush fill Corado's swarthy face at her touch. He glanced at her hand, clutching his arm, and then raised his eyes slowly to hers. When he finally spoke, his voice sounded thick.

"Very well, *señorita*. The Indian said a man on a chestnut stud had passed here last night. He seemed to be drunk. He shouted and fired at them with his pistol, and they ran into the forest. He rode off to the north."

El Sombrío had dropped off his horse and was hunting for tracks on the ground. He straightened up, looking surprised. "That is funny. These are of shod hoofs, and they head due west."

Carlota looked sharply at Corado. "Why should your Indians lie?"

Corado flushed. "They are not my Indians. Perhaps they were too frightened to watch closely."

"Are you still trying to spare me?" she asked. "Do you really mean that perhaps they belong to *los fantasmas en la noche?*"

There was a brittle tension in her voice, her face. It was what Hayward had sought to uncover when he had talked to her at the house, two weeks before. It let him see through the pride for the first time, let him see that the spectral fear of the *fantasmas* spared her no more than the others.

When Corado did not answer, she reined her bay around and drove it into the cañon. The others followed,

108

catching up with her. If the tracks headed west, as El Sombrío had said, there was no place they could go save straight up the cañon. Its walls were far too steep and rocky for a horse to climb. They pushed through the narrow gorge with the matted undergrowth clawing at them sharply to the high mesa above. And here, in the last tawny light of day, they saw Antonio's chestnut. It was cropping peacefully in a broad meadow of curing grass.

They rounded up the horse. Its saddle was still on, with no sign of violence about it. They scouted the meadows and timber about the spot until darkness fell, and then had to give up. They built a fire and cooked a meager meal. Corado said the trail would be cold by tomorrow, and would take them a long time to follow, and tried to get Carlota to go back. But she refused. Clouds hid the moon and did not leave them enough light to read sign by. They had to wait till morning, and finally rolled up in their blankets to sleep. Corado was soon snoring lustily, with the rest of them. But Hayward was restless, unable to settle down, thinking about Rodríguez and trying to guess how he fitted into this. Then a hand touched his shoulder. It was Carlota.

He followed her outside the circle of the dying fire, and she turned to speak in a low voice. "What do you think?"

"Maybe your brother was pitched . . . knocked unconscious."

"The chestnut is a cattle horse and would not have wandered far from a fallen man. He was drunk, Juan. He must have gone farther on foot. But we'll never find him if Corado keeps throwing us off this way."

"What's wrong with the man?" Hayward asked.

"He is trying to spare me, can't you see? Corado has been our *amansador* since I was a little girl. When we went riding, or to parties at other ranches, or took trips to town, Father always put us in Corado's care. Corado came to think of himself as a sort of guardian. He took great pride in it. Even more so since Father's death. And now he thinks something bad has happened, and he doesn't want me to be hurt. He may bluster and rage, and call this talk about the *fantasmas* the prattling of old women, but underneath I think he knows they exist."

"And you?"

She dropped her eyes, biting her ripe underlip. "I'm sorry I was that way in the house. But you were an outsider, Juan. I couldn't let you see all the troubles, the fears, the dirty wash. . . ."

He grasped her arm. "One of the things I admire about you most is that pride. Am I still an outsider?"

She looked up at him, cheeks satin-soft in the moonlight. "I can't think of you as one any longer. I need your help, Juan. I can't waste any more time fighting with Corado. I have one idea where Antonio might have gone. We are not too far from Higuera Cañon. The old Higuera Ranch is down there. Antonio and I knew it as children. Don Inocencio Higuera was a friend of my father's, and we went to his ranch often. If Antonio was drunk, and thought those Mutsune Indians were *fantasmas* or somebody trying to get him, he might have headed toward the Higuera Ranch. It's the only place around here that would give him any kind of shelter. Maybe he was pitched from his horse, lost it in the darkness, and went on afoot."

"How far is it?"

"Only a few miles from here. There is a definite trail. He might have followed it."

Hayward nodded, squeezed her arm, then sneaked back to get their horses. They saddled up out of earshot from

110

the camp and then rode into the darkness. They traveled for an hour, picking their way over the incredibly steep ridges, following a dim trail through the spired redwoods, the feathery cypresses. They reached the coast, the edge of a high cliff, and looked down at the snowy phalanxes of the surf throwing themselves forever against the impregnable rocks. There was something abandoned and passionate about it, like the shocking streaks of barbarism and passion that lay hidden beneath the deceptively golden surface of this land, of these people.

They rode on, following the cliffs. It was the same section Pío Tico and El Sombrío and Hayward had ridden that first time, following the man who had shot at Antonio. But Carlota knew a trail that cut off many extra miles. Finally they reached the mouth of Higuera Cañon, opening like a knife slash into the ocean, where Hayward had been unable to find a trail that would take the horses down. But she found one, farther up than he had looked, hidden in a snarl of brambles and scrub oak. They forced their way through the clawing brush, picked their precarious way to the dense-timbered bottom. The thunder of the sea crashed and echoed in the gorge.

Carlota led unerringly to the buildings in which Hayward had found Morgan the last time. It was black as pitch. No light showed from the windows; no horses stirred in the corral. Hayward lit a match and entered, finding the same broken lamp and lighting it. One of the trapper's pack saddles lay in a corner, and a torn pair of elkhide leggings still hung above the fireplace, but the place had obviously been vacated. And there was no sign of Antonio. Carlota's face went slack with both disappointment and relief. She stood in the center of the room, then, frowning to herself.

"Few people know this," she said. "These are the build-

111

ings of the second Rancho Higuera. The original house was built high on the bluffs on the other side of the cañon. It was abandoned early in the century because it was too inaccessible. I don't even think my father knew the old trail up. But one day Don Inocencio Higuera took Antonio and me up there. It was a frightening place, like a castle, set so high on the cliff. . . ."

She trailed off, raising her eyes to Hayward. He knew what she was thinking. "It's worth a try," he said. "No telling what crazy thoughts Antonio would get in that drunken brain of his, if he thought the *fantasmas* were still chasing him."

She looked at him a moment longer, the red of her lips almost black in the treacherous light. Then he blew out the lamp, and they went to their horses again. They went on down toward the sea till he thought they would ride right into the foaming breakers. On the bone-white sand of the beach she turned into the rocks of the cliff, following a ledge up through them that became a shelf twisting and turning up the face of the cliff. Higher and higher they climbed, with the surf snarling endlessly at the rocks beneath them. Hayward had only a sense of the height until the moon scudded from behind a cloud. Then he had a glimpse of the crashing sea a hundred feet below and grew so dizzy he had to turn in toward the cliff.

And still they climbed, until their horses were blowing for air and gleaming with sweat. They reached places where the trail had crumbled away and had to dismount and fight with the horses to get them across. Once Hayward's mount slipped, and he thought he was gone. But it scrambled to firmer ground, trembling in fear, and it took him ten minutes to coax it into movement again.

At last they reached the top, with the animals shudder-

112

ing in exhaustion beneath them. On their flank, not twenty feet back from the edge of the cliff, was the house. It was a huge, sprawling, tumbled old house with square towers and archways that had fallen in, the myriad tiles of its roof winking palely at the moon.

"Don Inocencio had the first winery around Monterey here," Carlota whispered. "And it was rumored that he smuggled goods in off of French and English ships when California was under the Spanish flag and was closed to foreign trade."

They got off their groaning horses and approached the house cautiously. They moved down the crumbling wall till they found a gaping doorway. They listened, and could hear nothing but the muffled cannons of the surf far below.

"There will be candles somewhere inside," she said.

"You wait here."

"Now you sound like Corado. We will both go in." She turned to fumble in her saddlebags. Then she came to him, the perfume of her hair in his nostrils, handing him a pistol.

"There is but one. You can probably do better with it than I."

For a moment he looked into her eyes and forgot where he was. Then he tore himself away, turned, and felt his way into the pitch-black room. She touched him, led him down the wall to one of the countless niches where these people kept their candles and their wooden saints. The first one was empty, and the second. The third yielded the dusty, rancid stub of a candle, which he lit for her. Its feeble glow bloomed across the room. The huge smoke-blackened beams had caved in at one end. Rubble was everywhere. A broken table was uptilted against one wall. They picked their way through the wreckage and found a hall. They stopped to listen. Suddenly Carlota drew a panicky breath.

113

"Antonio? . . . Tonito!"

Her voice rang down the hall, echoed hollowly through other rooms, and died. She turned sharply to Hayward, and he could see the pressure building up in her. He caught her to him with one arm.

"Take it easy."

"I'm frightened. I haven't let myself be till now, but suddenly I'm frightened."

He held her against him, feeling that ripeness of breast and thigh flatten to his body again. She was trembling, and she clung to him, biting her lip and fighting back tears, and he knew he had been right, it was something special — even under circumstances like this, it was something special.

"We'll find him now," he said. "If he's here, he's probably sleeping it off. We'll find him."

She looked up at him. "Is there never a time when you don't grin?"

"If you don't like it, I'll move right over to the mourner's bench."

"No." She touched his lips, and a smile quirked her own mouth. "I like it. I think it makes me feel better, somehow. Who could worry with you around?" She collected herself with an effort, pulled away. "Come. I've been foolish. Let's hunt."

He turned reluctantly and moved ahead of her through the hall. The boom of the surf sounded far away now. Rubble crumbled beneath their feet. A rat scampered across their path. Carlota stifled a cry. They passed into a bedroom, where cobwebs hung in streamers from the walls, out into a patio, across that into another hall. This led them into another huge chamber with a fireplace at both ends. Its gaunt windows opened out onto the cliff edge again, and the salt air came through to sting them.

114

They crossed the room, found another hall.

It was getting on Hayward's nerves, too, now. He heard Carlota breathing heavily just behind him. Ahead it was black as pitch. As Hayward reached the end of the hall and stepped out, there was a rattling scratch to his left.

The thought of a rat leaped into his mind again, but he couldn't help turning anyway. That was what saved him. He had just one glimpse of James Morgan's contorted face as the man lunged at him, and of the hatchet swinging down at him in a vicious arc.

He could only throw himself aside. The blade whirled past his head, and the handle struck down his arm. He dropped the candle, shouting with the stunning pain of it. The candle sputtered on the floor, and in its light Hayward saw the man wheeling around to strike again. He threw himself bodily at Morgan, his right arm still numb.

He knocked the man backward. Morgan's blow missed its mark, the blade ripping Hayward's jacket from neck to bottom. Hayward clawed for the man's axe wrist, got it, drove the man on back. The low sill of one of the open windows caught Morgan across the back of the thighs, and he flipped down into it. Unwilling to let go of the man's wrist, Hayward sprawled atop him, smashing for his face.

Morgan jerked aside from the blow, and their struggles carried them across the three-foot sill, tumbling to the ground outside. Still Hayward would not release that wrist as long as Morgan held the hatchet, and they rolled across the ground, grappling together. Morgan kicked over on top, trying to put a knee in Hayward's groin. Hayward blocked it, and Morgan fell heavily against him, pulling him farther over. Hayward saw that they were only a foot from the edge of the cliff and sprawled his legs wide to keep from falling over.

115

It lost him leverage to twist for a moment, and he could not avoid the blow Morgan smashed at his face. It stunned him, and Morgan's lurching struggle tore Hayward's upper body off the edge of the cliff. He had a dizzying glimpse of the surf far below, snarling at a thousand jagged rocks. He let go of Morgan and clawed wildly at the brush on the lip. Morgan jumped to his feet and shifted his weight to kick.

Hayward knew it would take only one solid blow to send him off. In the last instant, he let go his precious hold on the brush. He felt the earth crumbling beneath him, felt himself sliding off. He threw an arm up to catch the foot as it reached him, grunting with the kick. His hold on the foot was the only thing that kept him from being booted over. He twisted with his shoulders and heaved. Morgan toppled like a felled tree, somersaulting over Hayward and out into mid-air with a wild cry.

Hayward went, too, but caught again at the brush. There was a ripping of branches. Then it stopped, and he was left hanging head down over the edge, holding onto the chaparral with desperate hands. He felt the brush giving, knew that if he shifted an inch his weight would break the brush, and he would be pitched after Morgan. But he could feel the roots slowly pulling out, and, if he didn't move, he would be pitched anyway. In that helpless moment, he heard the tattoo of boots on the ground. It stopped, and he looked up to see Corado towering over him. For a moment the man hesitated, a blank look on his face. Then he dropped to a knee, bracing himself, and gave Hayward a hand.

It was nip and tuck till Hayward got his weight back on solid ground. He lay there, gasping for air, so drained he could not move.

"I woke to find you gone," Corado said. "I thought

116

Carlota might have the Higuera Ranch in mind. I followed you."

Hayward got to his hands and knees, crawling to the edge. Corado looked over with him. Far below, a black shape against the white sand of the beach, lay the inert body of the trapper.

"He does not move," Corado said. "A man does not fall that far and live."

From the house, they heard Carlota calling. Her voice had an hysterical sound. Hayward got to his feet, stumbled back to the window. He crawled through and groped around the room for the candle. He found it, lit it. With Corado behind him, he ran down the hall and through the door to the patio. Carlota stood by the crumbling, tile-roofed well, staring at him with wild eyes.

"It's all right," he said. "Everything's all right now."

She did not answer, staring in that half-dazed way at him. He saw the boots, then, protruding from behind the well. He moved out till he could see the man lying face down, with the big shining knife buried to the hilt between his shoulder blades. It was Antonio Mateo.

Chapter Ten

They reached Rancho del Sur near sunset on the next day. They had ridden all of the previous night to get Carlota back home. She was in a bad state of shock, so dazed and grief-stricken she would hardly speak. They put her to bed in care of her aunt and sent to Monterey for the doctor. Then Hayward and El Sombrío and the others went down to the peons' quarters and told the people what had happened.

"What of Corado?" Nieves asked.

"I brought Carlota on ahead so she would not have to ride with the body," Hayward said. "Corado will be along soon with Antonio."

Hayward was so weary, however, that he fell asleep long before Corado arrived. He awoke the next morning late, to find Nieves warming over his breakfast. He was only half through when Corado lumbered in, sitting heavily at the table across from him. He leaned his elbows on the planks, rubbing red-rimmed eyes. Finally he said: "The priest will come tomorrow. It will be a simple funeral."

"Why should Morgan have wanted to kill him?" Hayward asked.

"Who knows?" Corado growled. There was a dead silence. The fire spat. Corado took his fists out of his bloodshot eyes, glaring at Hayward. "Now, don't start talking about the *fantasmas* again."

"I didn't say a thing."

"You were thinking it. You're all thinking it. Damn it!" He jumped up, sweeping a cup off the table. He circled

118

around the room like an angry tiger, sending a neat pile of
firewood all over the floor with an angry kick. "Something
like this happens, and everybody goes crazy. Two of my
best men deserted this morning. More will be gone by evening. It was probably just a little fight. Don Antonio was
drunk, and he wandered up there and scared the hell out
of Morgan, and Morgan jumped him before he could think.
So what happens? The whole country turns upside down.
My crew runs off to the mountains, and the women are
hiding like mice in the houses, and I'll get the blame for
everything."

"Sit down and eat," Nieves said. "You'll feel better."

Cursing, Corado sat down. She put a plate of beef and
beans before him, and he began to eat, stuffing his mouth,
dribbling juice down on his chin, grumbling to himself.
Hayward had lost his appetite and so toyed with his food.
Finally, Corado raised sullen eyes to him again.

"Will you get it off your mind? Will you think about
something else? Let's talk about women or something."

"I wasn't thinking about Antonio," Hayward said.

"What, then?"

"Carlota."

Corado put his fork down. "What about Carlota?"

"Was what happened to Antonio what you were trying
to spare her?"

"How do you mean . . . spare?"

"You know what I'm talking about. Not wanting to talk
with those Indians, telling us they said north when they really said west, trying to send Carlota home."

A guilty look spread through the man's face. He
dropped his eyes, belched, played with his fork. "Do you
blame me?" he said, in a low voice.

"No. It was a terrible shock to her."

119

"His death would have been, anyway. But if only she hadn't seen it. . . ."

Corado broke off, staring blankly at the table, and after a while Hayward said softly: "She said you have been with the family a long time . . . ?"

"Most of my life," Corado replied in a muffled voice. "You don't know how it was, watching her grow up, teaching her how to ride, to shoot. . . ."

"I suppose you would develop a fatherly feeling."

"I am not *that* old." Corado sounded disgusted. "I was fifteen when the mission father turned me over to Don Fernando Mateo. Carlota was five. The old don . . . he taught me all I know about horses, spent more time with me than he did with his own son. Perhaps Don Antonio was a wastrel, a drunk, a fool. But he was not all bad. He had his charming side, and he meant a lot to Carlota. I knew what a shock his loss would be."

"Then, if you were trying to spare her, you must have suspected something had happened. All this bluster about the *fantasmas* . . . ?"

"Is just bluster," Corado conceded. "Of course. You must have guessed that a long time ago. Do you think I am a fool? I know my country better than that. I probably know more about the *fantasmas* than these old women who cower in their hovels spreading the rumors. And what if I stopped blustering? Do you think Rancho del Sur would hold together five minutes? Half the riders have deserted already. How many do you think there would be left if it were known that Miguel Corado admitted the existence of the *fantasmas,* and was afraid, too?"

"I suppose you're right. They do need someone to hold them together." Hayward frowned at him. "But you say you know of the *fantasmas* . . . ?"

120

The man shrugged, scowling at the table. "I have seen things up in the Santa Lucias. I have talked with Mutsunes who watch riders in the night that belong to no ranch. I know a man in Monterey who is marked, and who will die, sooner or later." He broke off, eyes lifting sharply, and then leaned back to laugh gutturally. "But you are too inquisitive for a man who has no reason to care. To sit around and mourn will not bring Don Antonio back. There is still work to be done. That horse will get rough if we do not keep at him. It is about time to put the bit in his mouth. What do you say?"

So they put the bit in his mouth. It was a big Santa Barbara spade bit with shanks six inches longs. They attached no reins to it. They merely set it in his mouth, attached to the headstall, and rode him around day after day with the hackamore reins for control, letting him get used to the feel of the iron against his jaws. The priest came from Carmel the second day, and they buried Antonio, and the ranch remained under a pall of gloom. Save for a brief veiled appearance at the funeral, Carlota stayed indoors. Hayward knew a need to see her, to help her somehow, but realized he could not force things. Time would have to heal the grief.

And Bardine was ever in his mind. Hayward worked at it constantly in all the little ways he had learned through the years, gaining the confidence of the men daily, putting together the rumors and the facts, the things they had seen in the mountains and the theories they had, waiting for another chance to renew the search. And all the time, the horse.

They had called it Cimarrón, which meant wild, for that's what he had been when they first found him.

Often, Pío Tico watched them from the fence, the

gleaming mahogany of his face stiff with rancor, his eyes shimmering with jealousy. It was like a small, insistent pressure against Hayward. But nothing happened. And two weeks after the death of Antonio, the roundup started.

Corado still would not let Hayward use the buckskin in his saddle string. The whole crew pushed deeply into the mountains and then spread out in units to gather in the cattle. Hayward, Gregorio, and El Sombrío got the section north of the Big Sur River. It was grueling work, sixteen hours in the saddle, fighting the steep mountains all the time, wearing down horse after horse. They got a gather and pushed it through to the holding grounds and went back for more. And all the time, they were working north. It was what Hayward had waited for. They finally made a camp in twisted badlands that he estimated were some five miles south of Rancho Higuera. And that night he sacrificed his precious sleep, stole El Sombrío's pistol from his saddlebags, and headed up the coast. But he soon came up against a cliff that ran right into the sea. There was no way up the sheer cliff, and he turned inland. He tried a half-dozen spur cañons that penetrated the cliff, but they all came to a dead end. He knew the escarpment must be the south wall of the mesa upon which the original Higuera house was built, but he could find no way through. And when he returned, near dawn, in weary defeat, he found that El Sombrío was not in his blanket.

He thought the man had trailed him, but El Sombrío did not return at breakfast time. Gregorio was not worried. He grinned knowingly.

"He will return tomorrow, or the next day. Always this happens when we get up in this section."

They rounded up more cattle and penned them in a brush corral at the dead end of a cañon. And that night El

Sombrío came back to camp, roaring drunk. Hayward could not understand where he would find liquor in this desolation. He did not even think there were Indians near enough to reach in that short a time.

El Sombrío only grinned slyly. "It is my secret," he said. "Enough wine to last me the rest of my life, and it is my secret."

He slept it off that night and was ready for work the next morning. No amount of probing would make him tell where he had got the wine. They took the new gather down to the holding ground and found that a bunch had been cut out to be driven to Monterey for the troops. In this country, any gathering was a good excuse for a party, and Colonel Archuleta always threw a big *baile* when the consignment of cattle was delivered. All the riders were looking forward to it, and the cattle were driven to town in a gay mood. Corado told Hayward to stop off at the ranch and get Cimarrón, for there was always a rodeo at these parties, and he thought the horse was about ready for a little competition.

After delivering the cattle to the barracks, Hayward rode with Corado and the rest of the crew to Colonel Archuleta's house, a massive two-story structure on a hill overlooking the town, its tile roof and long balcony barely visible through the grove of wind-twisted cypresses surrounding the place. Already the hitch racks were lined with proud, stamping horses, and there were a dozen buggies and coaches parked under the trees. At the corrals behind the house, riders from other ranches had already gathered. Cook fires were roaring, and whole pigs and quarters of beef were dripping on their spits. Hayward started to accompany Corado to the laughing, shouting crowd, when he saw Carlota appear at the doorway of the big house. She

123

beckoned to them, and they rode up. She was still dressed in black and her face was pale and drawn.

"Colonel Archuleta has invited the Americans in town," she said. "You are included, Juan."

Hayward glanced uncomfortably at Corado, who grinned broadly. "Do not worry, my friend. When you get tired of their sterile jokes and their genteel manners, come out with us and see a real show."

Laughing, he rode away with the other men. It was the first time Hayward had seen Carlota since the death of her brother. He felt stiff and awkward and did not know what to say. She saw his discomfiture and put her hand on his arm.

"It is all right. It has been long enough now. Just do not talk of it, and I will be all right."

They were ushered through the door by an Indian servant, stepping into the immense beamed living room that ran the length of the front. It was already crowded with people, swimming with the smoke of cigars and the penetrating scent of perfumed candles. A troubadour was wandering through the crowd singing a *cantinela*. On every side jewelry and silver winked and glittered in the firelight; the red and purple and blue of rich satins and silks dazzled Hayward's eyes.

Carlota introduced Hayward to Colonel Archuleta. He was a tall rawboned man dressed in the handsome blue uniform of the dragoons. He had thick black hair, tinged with gray at the temples, done up in a queue at the back of his neck. His face was burned dark by the sun, deeply lined, and, though his smile came and went with genuine warmth, the humor never touched his piercing black eyes. He bowed gallantly before Carlota.

"I hoped it would cheer you up after your loss. You

124

know, your father was my closest friend. It was as if I lost a son of my own," he said. Carlota dipped her head in thanks, and Archuleta did not press the matter further. "I am happy you came," he told Hayward. "You will find many of your countrymen here."

"Will he?" said *Alcalde* Rodríguez from the doorway. "One would almost think you were plotting a revolution, Colonel."

They all turned to see that the *alcalde* had just been ushered in. The man was dressed in blinding elegance. His hat was the bright yellow of imported Peruvian vicuña skin, his gold-embroidered jacket of padded red silk; linen gleamed like snow from the slash in his blue velvet pantaloons.

"Let us put aside our petty differences for the evening," Archuleta said, "and know the pleasure we enjoyed in the old days."

With a flourish, Rodríguez untied his cloak, and Ugardes caught it as it slipped from him. "I cannot blind myself to such dangers," he said. "I insist you remove the Americans."

Archuleta was still smiling. "And if I refuse?"

"I will have them removed."

"With my troops, *alcalde?*" Archuleta asked suavely.

Rodríguez turned a dull red. His lips pouted out, then compressed, digging creases in his heavy jowls. His breath left him in a spiteful hiss, like steam escaping. When he finally spoke, his voice shook with anger.

"Someday, Archuleta, you will not have your troops behind you. The reins will be in my hands, and we will see who laughs then."

He wheeled and stamped across the room. They saw him stop before a pair of men by the fireplace, say something, then look back over his shoulder at Archuleta.

125

"Already planning my downfall," chuckled the colonel. "Come, Hayward, I will introduce you to some happier people."

The Americans of the town were gathered by one of the punch bowls. The two Gilroy brothers stood together, stiff and uncomfortable in tall white collars and town suits. Callahan greeted Hayward with a bland smile. There were a British lawyer and a Scottish minister and half a dozen others, all greeting Hayward cordially. Yet beneath their cordiality he sensed an insistent tension; they pointedly ignored the politics of the town, discussing only crops and their home countries and the merits of the mission wines. The tables groaned with food. Salads of beets and cabbage and celery, *quelitas* cooked like spinach and fried with minced onions, and raisins and hard-boiled eggs; enchiladas of blue corn meal stacked on the table like huge pancakes; *empanadas* stuffed with tongue and currants and spices and wine.

After the meal, the orchestra struck up a quick *jarabe*, and the floor was filled with dancers. Out of respect for her brother's death, none of the young men was asking Carlota to dance. She talked with the older women for a while, then drifted to the punch table. Hayward followed, pouring her a glass. She sipped at it, eyes meeting his over the rim of the glass.

"Is it good to talk with your own people again?"

"I'd just as soon talk with you."

"Then let us go into the patio. It is stifling in here."

He took her arm, and they moved out into the patio. There were a pair of young lovers by the tile-roofed well. Hayward and Carlota wandered past them to the open gate. Here the heavy growth of jasmine on the wall hid them from the well and from the house. Carlota leaned

126

against the open gate, listening to the shouts and laughter of the men around the campfires outside. The black bodice of her dress lent sharp accent to the upper slopes of her breasts; they were white as snow and swelled seductively with each breath she took. It made him think of that kiss, so long ago.

"Corado says you are doing wonderfully with the buckskin," she murmured. "He thinks you have the makings of a true *amansador*. You are even learning to rope like one of our men."

He did not answer. He was studying her face, the soft curve of her cheek, the sparkle of her eyes. He was wondering if it was too soon after her brother's death.

The jingle of spurs broke into his thoughts, and he looked up to see one of the men from the campfires passing the gate. They could hear the new burst of sound down by the fires, the shouting and the stutter of hoofs. Carlota called to the man, asking him what was going on. He respectfully removed his hat.

"Some Indians have found a bear down by the Carmel River, *señorita*. Some of us are going to see if we can catch it."

A half smile touched her face. "Always something like that. Do you think us barbarous, Hayward?"

He shrugged, without answering, and she turned to him. "You are in a strange mood tonight," she said. "Where is the grin, the laugh? When you came to the ranch, everything was a joke. You were laughing all the time and making love to the girls and having such great times with Corado. Even when you kissed me that time, you were laughing. Why not now, Juan?"

It was like someone stirring hot coals in his belly again, and he knew he couldn't help it — even if it was too soon after Antonio's death, he couldn't help it. "Maybe it isn't a joke any more," he said.

"What isn't?"

He put his hands on her arms. The flesh burned against his palms like hot satin.

"This."

She did not fight him. Perhaps it was the scented night; perhaps it was the savage look on his face. But she did not fight. Her lips flared under his, and her young curves molded to him till he could not distinguish between the flesh of her body and the silk of her gown.

When it was over, they were both trembling.

She pulled back, staring up at him. There was no anger in her eyes. They were luminous, shining. He held her away. His heart was hammering, and he felt somehow that he had lost control of the whole thing.

"You are right," she whispered. "This time . . . it was no joke."

That was bad. A man couldn't afford to lose control. He had to keep it in relation. He told himself he had to keep it all in relation. A special one, maybe — but he'd had plenty of special ones before and had never lost control.

"Look," he said. "If it's too soon for that, I'm sorry. I didn't mean it to be too soon."

"Did I take my quirt to you?"

He couldn't help grinning. But it wasn't really funny. Somehow she was in control of the situation this time. He'd had it all his way before. But now he felt at a loss. He was still staring at her stiffly, uncomfortably, when they heard the husky voice rise from within the house, coming to them over all the other sounds.

"There are just three things, my friends. In all the world, just three things. Fighting and drinking and

128

wenching. Is there anything else? And who is better than Miguel Corado? Who can whip every man in Monterey bare-handed? Ten, twenty, fifty at a time, I don't care. And who can consume seventeen quarts of mescal between sundown and dawn, and walk out of it sober as a judge? And who, my friends, in all of Monterey, in all California, in all the world . . . who can wench like Corado? Why do the bulls in the pasture turn green with envy when I ride by? Why do the studs in the corral hang their heads in shame?"

Carlota took Hayward's arm, guiding him back through the patio and in the door. "They will allow him to stay only because of their regard for him," she said. "He is drunk and will shame us all. He must have wandered in looking for you. Only you can get him out without a scene."

"Why me?"

"You are his best friend."

"His what?"

"Don't you know . . . by now?" she asked. "Everybody else does. Why do you think he is taking such great pains with you and that horse? He wouldn't do that for anybody else. Does he spend so much time with El Sombrío, with Pío Tico? You have ridden with him, Juan . . . you have worked with him . . . you have fought with him as no other man ever did. It is those things that make a man his friend. More than just his friend. You know what *compadre* means in our language. It can't be translated very well into English. Not the feeling of it. Not the way a man would give everything for his *compadre*, even his life."

He gazed blankly at her, a little shocked by the revelation. He had felt himself close to Corado, in a rough, comradely way. But not anything like that. It was a little hard for him to assimilate, in that brief moment. He had trav-

129

eled so much in the last years, there had been little time to develop a friendship like that. He couldn't even recognize his own reaction. And he had no time to dwell on it. The man's voice was still booming, by the fireplace.

"Let me tell you of Serafina, my friends. There was a wench. I have never beheld anything like it. Do you know the pomegranate? Do you know how large they can grow? Imagine two of them, at their largest, like this. . . ."

Hayward drew near and saw Corado gesturing lecherously with his hands. The women were dipping their faces behind their fans, and the men were shifting uncomfortably in embarrassment. Archuleta's grin was half amused, half angry, as he tried to tug Corado away. But Corado was swaying with drink and did not seem aware of the man's urgings.

"Corado," Hayward said. "There is no one who can match you when it comes to fighting and drinking and wenching. But how about a bear?"

The man turned, blinking at Hayward, then grinned. "Juanito, I came looking for you. A bear?" He pounded his chest. "I have killed hundreds of them . . . bare-handed."

"They've found another one down by the Carmel River. Gregorio said you are too drunk to go after it."

"Too drunk?" The words left Corado in a roar. He lurched at the crowd, and it parted fearfully before him. His immense cartwheel spurs made a great clatter across the floor. "The drunker, the better. I am a seventeen-quart man."

Following him, Hayward saw relief on Carlota's face. She caught his arm as he went by, saying: "Go with him. See that he does not get hurt. Rancho del Sur would be nothing without Corado."

Hayward grinned reassuringly. "He'll be sober by the time we reach Carmel."

130

Chapter Eleven

There was a great stamping and snorting of horses about the fires. Since he had been in the country, Hayward had been told many stories of these grizzly hunts, and had always wanted to see one. He had heard how huge and ferocious the bears were, and it was hard to believe that these men were preparing to go out and get one without the aid of a gun. They were like a bunch of kids at play, whooping and hollering and racing their horses back and forth. One of them raced headlong past Hayward, tossing his rope at a fence post and snubbing his end tightly around a huge saddle horn. Another made a thirty-foot toss and plucked Corado's hat neatly from his head. Corado roared angrily at the man, and another rider raced by, leaning from the saddle to scoop the hat off the ground, passing Corado at a dead run and dropping the hat back on.

Pío Tico brought the black. He and Hayward had to lift the drunken Corado aboard. Then Hayward got his buckskin, and the three of them swung into the lead of the cavalcade as it filed out of the compound, skirted the shadowy town, and rode into the hills behind Monterey.

The Santa Lucias rose before them, dark, somber, with the haunted shapes of twisted cedar making feathery shadows against the moon. The Mutsune Indian who had found the bear was trotting at Corado's stirrup, and the other men, most of them drunk, were now riding close behind. Corado reeled heavily in the saddle, snapping white blossoms off the yuccas with his *tapaderos,* singing his song:

Ojos trigueños, color de café,
Dame un beso de buena fé. . . .

Deep brown eyes of coffee hue,
Give me a kiss, loving and true. . . .

They all joined in, rattling their bit chains and popping their quirts against rawhide leggings. There was a comradeship to it that got under Hayward's skin. It was one of the things he had sacrificed by working alone so long. He found himself joining in the song. Corado roared with laughter and slapped him on the back.

"You are a man after my own heart, Juanito. Never take life seriously. Always laughing, always making the joke. You should stay on after your sentence is up. It is not often I meet one like you."

"You're drunk tonight," Hayward chuckled. "Tell me the same thing when I make a mistake with Cimarrón."

"You know I will. I wouldn't get so mad with you if I didn't like you so much. Come on, now . . . sing."

Riding beside the sweating, drunken man, Hayward roared out the song. He was remembering what Carlota had said. *Compadre.* It had been a surprise, at first. Now he tried to analyze his reaction. Corado might have none of the civilized niceties. He might be primitive and violent, might have his savage appetites, his shocking lusts, his streak of brutality, of cruelty. But he was a man, clear through, with a blunt honesty, a zest for living, a reckless sort of courage that appealed to Hayward.

And Hayward knew suddenly that it needed no analysis. Friendship was a thing of sentiment that a man did not allow himself to consider too often. It required no explanation, no dissection. It simply existed. And Hayward realized

132

that Carlota was right. Corado was his *compadre*.

The Indian led them across the low hills, trotting tirelessly through the twisted cypresses and the shadowy pines to the Carmel River. Here, in the white sand beneath the moonlight, he pointed out the tracks.

"I never saw a bear that big," Hayward said. "Looks more like an elephant."

Corado rocked with laughter. "Callahan told me about the little brown bears you have back where the Yankee ships come from. This is something different, Juanito. Callahan . . . he calls it a grizzly. You will see. Never in all the world such a bear." He looked at Hayward's rope. "You only have forty feet there. You had better trade for my eighty-foot one. You don't want to get too close with that buckskin still under double reins. It won't be like roping in a corral. If that bear gets close enough to take a swipe, he'll knock off the whole back end of your horse with one blow."

So they traded ropes, and then started across the river. They climbed the bank on the other side and rode through heavy timber. They reached a meadow, surrounded by towering redwoods, with the moonlight sifting down through the gigantic trunks to paint the open park in broad yellow stripes. The bear tracks became plain here, about a berry bush that had been torn to shreds. A pair of Indians were waiting by a huge tree, and they pointed across the clearing, calling something to Corado.

"These bears often come down to feed on the carcasses of whales left on the beach by the Portuguese whalers," Corado said. "This one has gorged himself and is on his way back into the mountains. The Indians have been following him for us. They say he is stuffed and moves slowly. Don't let that fool you. When the time comes, he can move like lightning."

133

He waved his arm, and the men spread out. They did not cross the open meadow, but circled through the trees on both sides. They reached the other side of the meadow, and the Indians began to move more slowly, studying the ground, stopping before each thicket. There was a crashing, deeply within the timber. The Indians stopped. Corado put the spurs to his black and trotted it forward, holding the fretting horse on a tight bit. Hayward's buckskin began to snort and fight the bit, a nervous lather breaking out on its chest and shoulders. Hayward knew that the very smell of a bear would send most horses wild, and could not understand how these men expected to get close enough to the grizzly to rope it.

Suddenly there was a sullen rumbling, almost directly ahead. The Indians ran around behind Corado's fiddling black. With a great tearing of underbrush, the huge shape lumbered out into the forest lane. It stopped, sniffing the air, blinking nearsighted eyes at the men. It looked big as a horse to Hayward.

"Let's get him," bawled Corado, and put the spurs to his black.

The steed fought the bit, trying to spin away. But Corado drew blood with his spurs, holding it down with a tight rein. Squealing in anger and pain, the black charged straight at the bear, with Corado swaying drunkenly in the saddle. The grizzly wheeled with a deafening roar and crashed off through the forest.

Hayward touched Cimarrón with his spurs. The buckskin responded so instantly that Hayward was almost pitched off. It bolted away in a dead run, the first horse to start after Corado. He saw Pío Tico and Pablo and Gregorio racing behind him. But the buckskin pulled away from them, dodging madly through the trees to Hayward's frantic reining. Then he burst into the open, right on the churning black rump of Corado's horse. The grizzly was halfway across the meadow, running hard.

"Head him into that gully!" Corado shouted. "We trap him in the bottom."

The bear saw the narrow gully zigzagging across the meadow, and tried to veer away from it. But Hayward reined the buckskin onto the bear's flank, turning the beast back. The buckskin tried to whirl away from the hated bear smell, fighting the bit and whinnying wildly, but Hayward kept both the hackamore and bridle reins tight, using his spurs more than ever before. With a frustrated roar, the bear tried to leap across the gully. But he did not quite make it. The opposite bank crumbled under his weight, letting him slide back into the brush-choked bottom. Hayward's flanking run had left him behind, and he spurred the buckskin to catch up. Corado had been so close behind the bear that his horse leaped over the beast's head as it slid back into the gully, and Corado made his throw while he was directly above the grizzly.

The loop caught the bear's threshing right leg and snapped tight as Corado landed on the opposite side of the gully. The bear made a second leap at the bank, and succeeded in clawing its way out. Corado was running ahead of it, trying to take the slack out of the rope and spill the bear. But the lumbering grizzly tripped on the rope, snagged a leg, and rolled over.

Racing toward the gully, Hayward saw a thousand pounds of bone and muscle jerk Corado's rope tight. He saw the rawhide line whip taut, saw Corado's black horse jerk and skid with the shock, then saw the line snap in two.

Corado had swayed forward violently to compensate for that first violent jerk on the rope. But the breaking line re-

135

leased the horse suddenly, allowing it to plunge forward again, and the second shift took Corado completely off balance. He was too drunk to catch himself in time, and spilled off over the rear.

Hayward had not quite reached the gully when the bear rolled to its feet, saw Corado, and charged toward him. Corado rolled over, shaking his head dazedly. Hayward saw that the man was too stunned to rise in time, saw that none of the other horsemen were near enough to intervene. With a shout, he raked the buckskin with his spurs. Its headlong gallop became a dead run, and it leaped the gully. At the same time, the bear reached Corado. The man threw himself aside, and the first swipe of a gigantic paw only caught him a glancing blow — but one that nonetheless lifted him bodily off the ground and knocked him back ten feet.

The bear had to stop and whirl back to charge Corado again, drowning out all other sounds with its enraged roar. Hayward saw the man roll over and try to rise, and sag back against the ground again, and knew the bear would finish him this time. The grizzly was only five feet from Corado when Hayward ran the buckskin between them and tossed his rope.

He had a startling glimpse of that immense, shaggy beast. Its slavering red jaws were open wide, its savage teeth gleaming white in the moonlight, its little eyes glowing like coals. Then his loop was over its head, and he pulled both reins against the side of the buckskin's neck and dallied his end of the rope around the saddle horn at the same time.

The buckskin responded like a top, spinning on one heel. There was a violent jerk on the rope, a squeal of strained leather. But the cinch held, and the bear was jerked away from Corado so viciously that Hayward thought its neck had been broken.

For a moment the shaggy beast's enormous weight stopped the buckskin in its tracks, pulling the horse back on its haunches. Then the grizzly recovered, leaping for the horse.

Hayward reined Cimarrón aside once more. The animal's lightning response wheeled it away from the bear's rush with but inches to spare. Again the horse reached the end of the short length of dallied rope. Again there was that squeal of leather, that tremendous jerk on the whole saddle.

This time the bear was thrown, choking and gasping, clawing wildly at the rope about its neck. From out of the darkness the other riders were racing to help, shaking their loops out, leaping the gully. Corado had rolled over, shaking his head, shouting feebly at Hayward.

"Let out your rope, Juanito! Don't play him so close. *Válgame Dios,* you think you are a bullfighter or something?"

Hayward had dallied close that first time for a short length of rope that would jerk the bear away from Corado. Now he realized what a lethal thing he had done. With his end hitched around the saddle horn and the loop noosed tightly around the grizzly's neck, it was like being tied to the bear by a fifteen-foot rope.

He tired desperately to cast his dallies loose before the bear recovered. But the grizzly leaped to its feet, snapping the hitches tightly around the horn with its lunge against the rope. Then it wheeled and charged. The beast was on all fours, its thick legs churning, the edges of its golden coat turned to a shaggy halo by the moonlight.

Hayward used the spurs and reined the buckskin aside once more. The animal spun so quickly and so hard that

Hayward was almost pitched from the saddle. The bear plunged helplessly past the horse's rear and hit the end of the rope. The buckskin was pulled down to its rump once more by the abrupt yank and had to dance wildly to keep its balance.

Only now was Hayward fully appreciating the incredible responses trained into Cimarrón by its long apprenticeship on the hackamore, leaving its mouth so tender and velvet-smooth that it reacted instantaneously to the slightest touch of the bit. What made it even more marvelous was Cimarrón's instinctive fear of the bear. Hayward was fighting the buckskin with each turn, and still the horse reacted with a speed that left the bear flat-footed.

As the grizzly rolled over, the first rider raced by, making his toss. It was Pío Tico, leaning far out of the saddle in an attempt to snare a paw. But the bear swiped the rope away and came to its feet. Coughing, blinded by Hayward's strangling noose, it lunged wildly at the roaring sound of the buckskin's breathing.

Hayward spurred Cimarrón again, jerking both hackamore and bridle rein against the left side of the horse's neck. Cimarrón reacted with that blinding speed, lunging ahead, changing leads, spinning. The bear's lethal swipe again missed the horse's rump by inches.

Corado was running around the combat in a frenzy, bawling at the top of his voice: "Juanito, let go. You can't keep playing him so close. That isn't a trout on the end of your line. It's a thousand pounds of killer. Let those dallies out. Give yourself more rope!"

Again Hayward tried to tear the hitches loose from his saddle horn and get more line between himself and the grizzly. But the bear spun after him too fast, rearing up over the horse.

For an instant, Hayward seemed suspended beneath that row of glittering claws on the bear's forepaws. But he had already reined the horse aside. It spun away as the bear came down, carrying Hayward from beneath the talons. The bear struck the ground with its forepaws a foot behind Cimarrón's churning rump. It roared with fury, then the roar became a squall as the rope snapped tightly about its furry neck once more.

Before the jerk could spill it, the bear lunged after Cimarrón. Again Hayward had to use reins and spurs. The horse spun aside so violently it almost jerked him from the saddle. The bear lunged by and hit the end of the rope. It tumbled onto its back, pulling the horse to a dead stop again, Cimarrón dancing beneath Hayward to keep its feet.

As the bear rolled over for another charge, Gregorio and El Sombrío raced in and made their tosses. Gregorio's rope snagged a hind leg, tripping the beast and spilling it again. Other riders were swarming in then, and the air was full of ropes, and the other legs were soon snared. They stretched the wildly thrashing grizzly on its back, like a hide on a frame. Hayward finally got his dallies unhitched and handed the loose end of his rope to another rider, so his horse could take a rest. The animal was heaving and blowing with exhaustion from the violent battle, covered with a dirty yellow lather. Corado ran over and pulled Hayward bodily out of the saddle, shouting and clapping him on the back, dancing around him like a child.

"*Dios,* what a bear fight! Why do we even bother taking it in for the bull, now? They can't ever match this. Did you see him, Tico? . . . did you see our Juanito? Right down the bear's throat. So close he could count his tonsils. And that horse . . . *Madre mía,* that horse! I told you we had a dream there, Juanito. Did you see him, Gregorio?

139

Dancing like he was at a ball. Playing that bear like a fish on a line. No other horse could have kept his feet like that. Not even my black. You saved my life, Juanito, you and that heavenly horse. Nobody else could have done it."

So worn out he was swaying dizzily on his feet, Hayward laughed huskily at the man. "You're so excited you forgot that swipe the bear took at you. I thought he tore off your whole side."

Corado slapped that side with a disgusted sound. The shirt was torn and a little blood-stained at its edges, but that was all. "It takes more than a grizzly to kill Miguel Corado, my friend. I was whirling away, and he just grazed me."

Suddenly that violent, childish transition of mood gripped Corado. All the humor left his face, and it grew dark with suspicion. He wheeled and walked over to his own rope, still attached to the bear's leg. Its end was dancing and snapping with the bear's struggles. He caught it up, flirted some slack down its length till the noose was loosened about the bear's forepaw, then flipped it free with a practiced snap of his wrist. He carried it back to Hayward, staring at the end that had broken.

"What is it?" Hayward asked.

The riders who had no ropes on the bear were gathered around them now, and they fell silent. Corado spoke in a low, husky voice. "How does that look to you?"

Hayward examined it closely. "Pretty frayed."

"Like it was broke?"

Hayward gazed inquiringly at him. "Are you thinking of Carlota's father?"

"Don Fernando was killed when his rope broke," Corado said. "Somebody cut it so it would not bear the strain."

140

"But we traded, don't you remember? This was my rope."

"That's what makes me wonder," Corado said. He was looking strangely at Hayward. "Why should anybody want you dead?"

A restless murmur ran through the men. Hayward found his eyes moving for an instant across their faces, stopping at one. Pío Tico stared enigmatically at him, his face as dark, as polished as some tropical wood. And Hayward was remembering El Sombrío's warning: "Tico would do almost anything to get back into the favor of Corado."

Slowly, as if by some volition outside his own, Hayward's eyes moved to the great, struggling beast on the ground with its slavering jaws, its taloned paws that could tear a man apart with one swipe. A chill ran through him. It was a great effort to grin.

"You're making it too dramatic. This rope doesn't look as if it's been cut."

"Doesn't it?" Corado asked.

Chapter Twelve

After they rounded up the black horse for Corado, he would not let Hayward work the buckskin any more, saying the horse had shown them what it could do and was too tired to risk further. So Hayward watched while they let the grizzly gain its feet. It rushed to the right, and the riders on the left jerked their ropes and tripped it. Then they let the beast rise again. It rushed to the left, and the riders on the right snubbed it down. They fought for an hour, the horsemen taking relays on the ropes, until the beast could be guided. Then Corado rode in front, letting out his rope to snap the bear's nose. The grizzly roared, lunged at him, and the march was on. Every few yards, Corado had to ride back in and tease the grizzly into another rush. Finally it lay down and refused to budge. They worked an hour, prodding and teasing, to get it up again.

At the Carmel River, it broke a rope, and two men almost got drowned putting another line on. A mile farther, the grizzly bit two lines apart and almost escaped. There was a wild flurry for a few minutes, until they hitched the loops on it again.

Little by little, teasing it, prodding it, tugging it, cajoling it, they moved the beast along. The chase had been exciting to Hayward. Now, however, the full implications of this sport were becoming clear to him. He suddenly found that he could not join in with the gaiety of the laughing, joking men.

It was mid-morning before they reached Monterey with the grizzly. The men were drooping in the saddle, red-eyed from lack of sleep, exhausted from their constant battle with the beast, but still keyed up by the excitement of the dangerous game, the anticipation of the future.

Riders had already gone ahead to tell the people, and there was a great crowd gathered around the bull and bear pit behind Callahan's Pacific Building. It was a big depression dug into the ground, twenty or thirty feet in diameter, with a high chalk rock barricade behind which the crowds could stand. The riders dragged the bear in, and another group brought a wild blackhorn bull from the military herd at the *presidio*. They roped the bull and held it while Corado shackled one end of a long chain to its leg. Then they stretched the bear out, and he shackled the other end to its leg.

Corado jumped back and gained the safety of the barricade. The riders then threw their ropes free and followed him. The bear rolled over, with a loud rattle of the chain, and faced the bull. Hayward saw the ring of excited, sweating faces press nearer the barricade, waiting for the first rush. Everyone was betting on how long the bull would last, or on which animal would draw first blood, or a dozen other possibilities.

Hayward saw Rodríguez and Colonel Archuleta and many other members of the party the night before, but could not see Carlota in the crowd. Over at the rear door of his building, Callahan was busy taking bets from a whole crowd of men. Then the bull bellowed and made the first rush. With a wild shout, the circle around Callahan broke up, and everybody ran to the barricade.

The bear dodged the bull, swiping out with his paw. He caught the bull on the shoulder, ripping off a long strip of hide. The bull wheeled, tossing its wicked horns, dripping blood. Hayward hung back from the circle of shouting, avid

143

watchers. He saw Callahan wandering over his way, counting money.

"You might say hello," the Irishman remarked.

Hayward glanced around, saw that nobody was within earshot. "You told me to keep away."

"I meant not to lose your head and come running at the first crack out of the box," Callahan said. "But you will have to admit it would seem funny if two of the few remaining Americans here didn't speak to each other when they met in town."

"I suppose you're right."

"You don't seem to like our sport," Callahan said.

"It seems cruel."

"And you wouldn't have gone to help drag that bear in if you'd fully realized what it meant?"

"I guess that's the way I feel."

"Where's that grin? I thought it was all a joke to you."

"We all have our bad moments."

"This can be a brutal land," Callahan told him. "You'll have to get used to our customs." He moved closer. "Find out anything?"

"I know for sure they were holding Roger Bardine up at the old Higuera place," Hayward said. "A man named James Morgan was mixed up in it. He was also there when Antonio Mateo was killed. Could that mean the *fantasmas?*"

Callahan put the money away and brought out his cutty pipe, frowning studiously. "Might be. Morgan's a renegade. Came down out of the Sierras about a year ago with a couple of other trappers. Caused a lot of trouble here in town. Finally the decent Yankees had to kick him out to protect themselves. Corado told me you killed him."

"It was either he or I."

Callahan's look was quizzical. Then he dipped his face

to light the pipe. "So that leaves us Bardine, still out there somewhere?"

"Could it still be the Higuera place?"

"Not now, not if you almost had them there twice."

"How about Bardine's daughter?" Hayward asked. "She suspects I've been sent here to find him. Is she a safe risk?"

"I'd say no. She's a half-breed, Hayward, and she's always been wild. Not actually a bad girl, but Bardine never had much control over her." Pipe smoke wreathed Callahan's face. "We've talked enough now. *Alcalde* Rodríguez is watching."

Hayward frowned at the man, then started to move away. Before he could do so, however, Corado ran up to place a bet with Callahan. Behind him the crowd was shouting wildly. The roars of the beasts made an unholy din in the pit.

"Five more *pesos* on the bear, Callahan." Corado's face was greasy with sweat, his eyes varnished with excitement. "He's going to get that bull yet. Did you see his trick? Clawing the nose. He's a smart bear. He uses his head." Corado grabbed Hayward by the arm. "What's the matter, Juanito? A little bloody? You'll get used to it. The good part is yet to come. The bull is hot with thirst. Sooner or later he opens his mouth and sticks out his tongue. Then the bear grabs it and eats it. You've never hear such a roaring."

Without waiting for an answer, Corado whirled back and ran to the barricade, shouting like a child at a circus. Hayward glanced at Callahan, then turned and went inside the Pacific House. There was nobody within the long, gloomy taproom. Exhausted from the all-night ride, he slouched into a chair behind a corner table, hoping no one would come in for a while. A great roar went up from outside

145

again. He couldn't tell if it was the people or the beasts. Then an elephantine shadow broke into the rectangle of light cast over the floor by the open door. It was *Alcalde* Rodríguez. Six feet inside, he saw Hayward and stopped, pouting his thick lips in irritation.

"What's the matter?" Hayward said. "You look sick."

Rodríguez moved peevishly to a table across the room, lowering his bulk into a chair. "I'll admit it," he said. "This part always makes me sick. I can't watch it."

"You must have a little Yankee blood, too."

The man turned sharply to Hayward, suspicion coloring his eyes. Then he said: "No Yankee blood."

"What kind of blood?"

"Spanish, you fool." Rodríguez yanked up one sleeve, pointing to the skin of his underarm. "Doesn't that prove it? White as snow. Castilian clear through. Not a drop of anything else."

"Not a drop of Indian blood?"

The man stiffened a little in the chair. There was a faint stir at the rear door. But Hayward had already seen Ugardes there, standing silently, in his red buckskins, with his cat's eyes.

"Are you insulting me, *señor?*" Rodríguez asked. His voice was brittle. "Do you forget that I have it in my power to order your execution?"

"No offense, *Alcalde.* Somebody just told me you were a peon once. Pulled yourself up by your bootstraps. You should be proud of that."

Rodríguez seemed about to speak again. But a roaring swelled from outside once more, checking him. He half turned that way. He moistened his lips.

"Has the bear got the tongue yet?"

Ugardes turned to look. "Not yet."

146

As Rodríguez wheeled around toward Hayward again, another man stepped into the open front door. He was silhouetted there, black against the blinding sunlight. It was the silhouette of a big man, with remarkably broad shoulders, long, solid legs. Before Hayward could make out his features, he stepped into the room. He was not a silhouette any more. He was James Morgan.

It hit Hayward like a blow to the stomach. Vaguely, he was aware of Rodríguez, bending forward, gripping the edge of his table, staring. Even Ugardes showed surprise. The shock of it receded like a tide in Hayward, leaving the nausea of reaction. The flesh of Morgan's face was brown as saddle leather, and his grin put a million wrinkles in it.

"Ain't this fancy, now?" he said. "Just the four of us."

"Morgan," Rodríguez asked breathlessly. "What is it? Was Corado lying to me?"

"Did he tell you no man could live through a fall like that?" Morgan asked. He was looking at Hayward.

"Of course," Rodríguez said. "Carlota said the same thing. She said the cliff was fifty feet high."

"I should know," Morgan said. "I crawled back up every one of those feet with sixteen broken ribs in my body." He came on into the room at a dragging walk, reaching a table, leaning against it. His eyes were fixed on Hayward. "I been clawed apart by grizzlies, mister. I been tortured by Indians and beaten to a pulp by white men and dragged ten miles on my belly behind the horse of a Mexican general, but none of it hurt as bad as this."

"Next time don't go so near a cliff," Hayward suggested sarcastically.

Anger made a raw stain against Morgan's cheeks. He had one hand splayed out against his side, held there tightly. It covered the hilt of his hatchet, thrust nakedly through his leather belt. He straightened up with an effort.

Rodríguez watched with fascinated eyes as Morgan moved in that dragging walk to the next table, six feet nearer Hayward. He leaned against it with one hand, still holding the other against his side.

"I made it down to one of them small ranches on the Salinas," he said. His voice came with hoarse effort. "They sent for the doc. He said I must have a little grizzly in me. No human could survive such a thing. I told the doc to keep it quiet. I was in bad with the *alcalde*. He might take advantage of me. The doc said he wouldn't say anything till I got on my feet."

"Morgan. . . ."

"Shut up, Rodríguez," Morgan said. He spoke to Hayward again. "But I didn't care about the *alcalde*, did I? I just didn't want you to hear. Not till I could tell you myself. That's what I thought about all the time, mister. Sitting in that shack, hurting more than I ever hurt before, just thinking of you."

"Rodríguez," Hayward said. "Are you going to arrest this man now?"

Rodríguez looked blank. His pouched eyes ran to Morgan. The trapper stood leaning against the table, wheezing softly. Something sly entered the *alcalde*'s face.

"Arrest him? What for?"

"For the murder of Antonio Mateo."

Rodríguez settled into his chair, pursing his lips. "What is your story, Morgan?"

"After Hayward caused us trouble that first time," Morgan said, "we moved our base to that big house up on the bluffs. We went out to work our trap lines every day. That day we came back and found Antonio Mateo's body. We got no idea how it come there . . . who brought it . . .

148

nothing. Then we heard somebody coming and doused the lights. Figured it was Mateo's killers. When they jumped us in the dark, it was natural we should fight."

"What do you mean *we?*" Hayward asked. "You were the only one there."

Rodríguez spread his hands. "We are at a stalemate, then. Your word against his, Hayward, and you already a prisoner. How can I believe you? How can I arrest him? Isn't that true, Ugardes?"

The man at the rear door smiled enigmatically, slipping the long knife from his leggings. "That's true," he said, touching the tip of the knife with his finger. "How can you arrest him?"

An enormous roar went up from outside. This time it came from the animals, and it was filled with the insanity of pain. Rodríguez moistened his lips again. Sweat made a greasy shine on his forehead.

Morgan waited till the sound had died down, then dragged himself to the next table. Only one table stood between him and Hayward now.

Hayward saw how it was. He had made a mistake taking a table in the corner. Ugardes blocked him off from the rear door. Morgan from the front. And he knew his slightest move to rise would bring Morgan at him with that hatchet. The man would trap him beneath the table before he could even get out of his chair. He had only one possibility left. All the time he had been sitting with his right hand on his knee, beneath the table. It had been that way even when Rodríguez entered.

"How will you explain this?" he asked Rodríguez.

The *alcalde* spread his hands helplessly. "A wild man . . . a man delirious with pain . . . wreaking vengeance. How could we stop him? We were over on the other side of the room when it happened. And we were helpless."

Another insane bawling rose deafeningly from outside. Morgan gathered himself and moved past that last table and reached Hayward's table. He leaned against it with one hand, still holding his side with the other. He was wheezing with the effort. The hand on Hayward's lap was knotted into a fist. It was all he had left.

"You'd better go," he told Morgan. "If the Mateo crew finds you in here, they'll tear you to pieces."

Morgan leaned toward Hayward. "I got something to do before I go. I been thinking about it so long, it seems I've wanted to do it all my life. And, by God, now I'm going to do it."

"Morgan!"

Hayward said it sharply. It stopped the man, for just that instant. He straightened up, the hatchet half pulled from his belt. Hayward sat woodenly, trapped between table and wall. He had not moved an inch. That very fact must have been what checked Morgan, what made him suddenly aware that one of Hayward's hands was invisible.

"I've got a pistol pointing at you," Hayward said. "If you lift that hatchet, I'll shoot."

Morgan's eyes blinked. He stared at the table. His fist closed against the handle of his hatchet till the knuckles turned white. His voice sounded strangled.

"Rodríguez, is that true?"

The *alcalde* frowned, started to change his position. "I cannot see."

"Don't try," Hayward said. "If anyone moves, I shoot." Ugardes had started to shift his weight, as if to walk in farther. Now he stopped. They all stopped, held by the threat in Hayward's words. Then Hayward said: "If I have no protection from the law, Morgan, neither have you. To

150

Carlota's people, you are the murderer of Antonio Mateo, whether it can be proven or not. If I shot you dead now, there wouldn't be a man in this town to raise a finger against me. So are you going to get out, or do I have to finish the job?"

A baleful look came into Morgan's pale eyes. Hayward could almost see him weighing his chances. Rodríguez watched him with that bird-like fascination in his eyes. The sound gathered like a storm outside and then ran thin and died. Finally the tension ran out of Morgan's body. Defeat made his face slack. Slowly, wheezing heavily, holding his aching side, he began to back up. For the first few paces he kept trying to see under the table. But it was too low. He stopped again.

"All right," he said. His voice was thick and shaken with frustrated rage. "There'll be other times. There'll be plenty of other times."

He stared at Hayward a moment, then walked out.

Hayward felt his body go slack in the chair with reaction. A tremor ran through him. Rodríguez took out a lace handkerchief, wiping his brow.

"I thought for a moment he would throw that hatchet, anyway."

"It was nip and tuck," Hayward said.

Rodríguez leaned confidentially toward him. "It would be useless for you to tell of this."

"You mean your alliance with Morgan?"

"No one would ever believe you."

Without answering, Hayward put his right hand back on the table. He saw the *alcalde*'s pouched eyes widen.

"*¡Señor!* You had no pistol."

Hayward grinned. "No one would ever believe you."

151

Chapter Thirteen

They returned to the ranch the day after the bull and bear fight. For a few days nothing happened. Hayward saw nothing of Carlota. He wondered if she were deliberately staying away from the corrals, deliberately avoiding him, trying to evaluate what had happened to her. He could understand that. Because he wanted time to think it over, too. It was easier, out of her presence. He seemed to lose all sense of proportion when she was near.

Maybe that was it. Just something that seemed bigger than it really was. He had thought he had been in love before, once or twice, but it had turned out sour. He could handle that. He told himself he could handle it if he watched his step, kept it all in its proper place, didn't succumb to the night and the scent of jasmine and those great big eyes. He could handle it, he assured himself.

It was four days after the party when Corado told him it was time to take the hackamore off Cimarrón entirely. He had shown them what he could do on the bear hunt, and it was time for the final stage of his training. They were out in the pasture, with the buckskin running in only the bridle, teaching the horse to cut cattle, when they got word that Carlota wanted to see them at the big house.

There was a pair of strange horses before the door, sweat-stained and travel-weary. Hayward followed Corado into the living room, and the first thing he heard, before he saw the men, was the twang of Yankee voices. Then his eyes became accustomed to the gloom, and he could make out the two men sitting at the end of the room. One of them was Lieutenant George Templeton. The man came to his feet, as surprised as Hayward.

"John Hayward!" he said.

Carlota looked surprised. "You know each other?"

"Know each other?" Templeton laughed. "Four years at West Point."

Carlota frowned at Hayward. "You were in the American Army?"

Templeton saw the expression on Hayward's face, and the humor left him. "I'm sorry, John. I didn't mean. . . ."

"It's all right," Hayward said. He saw Corado watching him suspiciously, and he knew he had better make it very clear. "I was court-martialed," he said, with just the proper amount of defiance.

"It wasn't really that bad," Templeton said. He looked uncomfortable now and was trying to make up for his slip. "John was just a little unorthodox for the Army. Always running against tradition at the Academy, maybe spending a little too much time with the ladies. In a war they would have made him a general. He just had the bad luck to run up against an old mossback at Leavenworth before his true talents were recognized."

"A lot more than that," Hayward said. "We might as well admit it."

He was grinning, but it still stung a little underneath. There had been a full court-martial, the shaved head, the drums rolling, all of it. Well, maybe it would have come about anyway. He'd been a little too wild, a little too gay. They had already warned him enough times. So the Torres plot had come up in Mexico City, requiring a man of his peculiar qualifications quickly, and they'd given him his choice. Either a real dismissal for all the trouble he'd caused them, or a sham court-martial for publicity and a

153

trip to Mexico City still in the pay of the Army, with everybody thinking of him as a disgraced officer, bitter against the United States, ripe for enlistment in just such a plan as Torres was hatching.

It had worked too well. After Mexico City, they had needed someone in Santa Fé, and after that Tripoli. But now, despite the sting, he was glad for it. If Templeton had suspected a thing, he would have shown it, and Hayward would have been through here. Frémont was one of the few who knew the truth, and apparently he had kept his mouth shut.

"You seem to have got over it," Templeton said.

Hayward grinned. "You know me."

"Did he ever take anything seriously?" Carlota asked.

"Never," Templeton said. He was a tall young man, sandy-haired, ruddy-faced. He wore Army blues, but they were almost white with dust and long wear. The sergeant behind him was a square-bodied, competent-looking trooper with saddle leather for skin, eyes the color of saber steel, and hair cropped close to his head.

"Lieutenant Templeton and Sergeant Parker are here from Captain Frémont, Juan," Carlota said. "We thought they had left the country, but apparently Frémont is still somewhere in the Sierras. My father was always friendly toward Americans and helped Frémont when he was here before. They knew they could safely come to me with their offer."

Templeton hitched thumbs in his belt, chose his words carefully. "It's sort of a two-way deal, John. The Americans will gain by it if it's successful, and the Californians who are against Rodríguez will gain by it, too. Naturally we're interested in breaking the blockade. The cobblers back on the Eastern seaboard had actually begun to depend so

154

heavily on California hides for their shoes that their production was cut almost to nothing when the hides stopped coming. And these people here are beginning to feel the pinch, too."

"It's true," Corado said. "My men have very little powder and lead left for their guns."

Carlota nodded. "It is not only the simple little luxuries they bring us, but we have come to depend upon them for actual necessities . . . medicine, needles, thread."

"That's why we've come," Templeton said. "We were at San Diego in May. Captain Lansing pulled in on the *Noah*. He said he was heading north and would be here late in June. He'd lie off the point south of Santa Cruz, and, if some rancher wanted to get a shipment of hides out to him, he had a whole holdful of trade goods to pay for them."

"Rodríguez has made it a serious offense to smuggle hides out," Carlota said. "But we need this too badly. I will not order you to get the hides, Corado, for it might mean jail. It might mean worse, if you were caught. I am simply asking you."

Corado looked at Hayward, then grinned broadly.

"And you have my answer. We will do it."

Chapter Fourteen

It took a lot of preparation. After Templeton and the sergeant left, Corado went back to the corrals, gathering only such men as he could trust, telling them the situation. More cattle had to be rounded up. The crews were immediately dispatched into the mountains. They were to drive the beef in small bunches to the holding ground north of Monterey, near the spot where the *Noah* would anchor.

It was doubtful if *Alcalde* Rodríguez could get Colonel Archuleta to move against them with his troops, even if what they were doing was discovered. But the Rodríguez adherents in town far outnumbered the Mateo crew, and could defeat them if it came to a showdown. So Carlota went to stay with the Archuletas in town. It would arouse no suspicion, as they were old friends and often visited each other. And she would be in a position there to watch Rodríguez and warn Corado if the *alcalde* discovered their hide operation.

Hayward rode with Gregorio and two others. But he was working under pressure now. Lansing was back with the *Noah*, and Hayward hadn't found Bardine yet. There would only be a few days left to find the man, and he had no definite leads. It would be tantamount to failure to reach the man after the *Noah* had sailed, for there would be no safe place to take him. Hayward realized by now that anyone might be a *fantasma*. There was no telling how large they were in numbers. There might be one in Monterey, a dozen, a hundred. Perhaps even some of the Mateo crew belonged to the group. So if Bardine were freed, he would still be a marked man. The only answer was to find him before the *Noah* sailed. But how?

It took Hayward and the crew he rode with a full day to gather a hundred Mateo steers in the mountains south of Monterey, and another day to drive them to the holding grounds on the upper curve of the bay, fifteen miles north of the town. Already other crews had brought in their cattle, and the herd filled the flats above the beach with their lonesome bawling, stirring the dust till it lay in a yellow fog against the sun.

Hayward and Gregorio drove their bunch into the main herd, then rode to the cook fires for something to eat. Hayward was surprised to see Aline Bardine at one of the giant stew pots, stirring chili and beans with a long wooden ladle. She wore a sleazy cotton dress that clung tightly to the buxom swell of her breasts, the lush curve of her hips. But, somehow, the healthy animal vitality of her did not reach him as it had before. He wondered if it was because of what had happened between him and Carlota. Or Callahan's warning. He was looking for the wildness Callahan had talked of. Aline looked hardly capable of it, with her unruffled calm, her bland peasant beauty. Yet there was something lurking in her eyes.

He realized she was probably one of his last hopes. Should he trust her now, tell her who he really was, on the off chance that she might give him some new bit of information that would lead him to her father? But what could she tell him? She had already admitted she didn't even know why they had taken Bardine. Besides, there was one basic rule on a job like this, and he had learned it the hard way. You could really trust nobody but yourself.

"I'm surprised to see you here," he said.

"Why?" she asked. "I offered to help. I will do anything

157

I can to defeat Rodríguez. This will be a blow to his prestige. If enough ranchers can smuggle their hides out, the embargo will be useless." She filled his plate and poured him a cup of bitter black coffee. Then she gave him a sidelong glance. "I understand Morgan was there again, when you found Antonio's body."

"That's right," he said.

"Do you think he led the *fantasmas?*"

"Do you?"

She pouted sullenly. "All right. I shouldn't have asked you anyway. I know now you couldn't be the one they sent in to find my father. You're no better than the rest of these *californios.* Lying around in the sun all day, snatching at every woman that goes by. Everything's such a big joke."

Angrily she ladled beans onto another plate and carried it over to Corado. He was sitting against one of the oxcarts and had just finished one plateful. He took the other from Aline without even looking up at her and began to stuff himself. Then he became aware of her bare brown legs so near to him, and looked up, wiping chili from his lips with a careless backhand swipe.

"What the hell are you standing there for?" he laughed.

She started to answer, but he grabbed her and pulled her down across his lap. He fondled her, kissed her, then, just as suddenly, he pushed her away. She rolled off his lap into the dirt.

For just a moment her eyes flashed with a tantalizing hint of the wildness Hayward had been watching for. It came and went too swiftly to analyze, and then she rose, brushing the dust from her dress. Corado got to his feet also, belching, laughing roughly.

"I have had the food and the love. Now it is time to go back to work."

158

He saw Hayward and hailed him, and went toward him. Aline stood where he had left her, staring fixedly after him. Her eyes were smoldering and heavy-lidded, her underlip ripe and full. It was a strange look, close to anger. Corado clapped Hayward on the back.

"I know you are tired, but we have to go right to work. This is going to be a *nuqueo*, Juanito. It's the way we slaughter when we are in a hurry. We haven't time to rope each beef out and kill it in the ordinary way. If Rodríguez gets a whisper of this, we will be through. So we have to do it fast. *Nuqueo* takes a good man. But after the way you handled that grizzly on the bear hunt, I think you can do it. And it takes a good horse, so put your saddle on Cimarrón."

Hayward saddled the buckskin, then Corado told him to take off his jacket and roll up his sleeves, and handed him a long knife. He saw Pío Tico and Gregorio and a dozen others in their shirt sleeves, each with a long knife. Corado rode to the herd with him, halted him near the fringe, while the others moved on in.

The half-wild blackhorns were just familiar enough with men and tired enough from the roundup not to stampede. Pío Tico maneuvered in beside a brindle bull. It happened so fast Hayward could hardly follow it. Tico's knife flashed in the sun. The blade sank to the hilt in the bull's neck. The beast roared in pain, its whole body stiffened spasmodically, then it dropped to the ground. The other men were striking, too, and more and more cattle were falling. Corado squinted at Hayward to see his reaction.

"Are you going to get sick again?"

Hayward knew Corado was thinking of the bull and bear fight and said: "That just seemed so unnecessary."

"*This* sure isn't unnecessary," Corado replied. "All of

159

California is based on cattle. I don't think we'd be here if it weren't for beef. There isn't a part of that animal we don't use. Eat the meat, sell the hides, use the fats for soap and grease, the tallow for candles, hair for rope, even make chairs out of the horns." He spat dust from his mouth. "You want to try, or are you too squeamish?"

"You need me, don't you?"

"Need every man I can get, if we mean to clean this up before Rodríguez finds out."

"Then I'll try."

"Get going, then. You want to learn how to strike before the herd starts running. Everything goes crazy then."

Already the growing stench of blood in the air was making the herd restless. Pío Tico maneuvered in beside a dun heifer, and she started to bolt. He had to spur his horse after her to strike. Corado pointed out a red cow to Hayward.

"Go in easy. Strike right at the nape of the neck. You have to get the blade between the bones."

Hayward reined Cimarrón in on the red cow's flank, saw her begin to stir. The stench of sweat and dust rose up from her hairy hide, almost gagging him. His knee touched her shoulder, and she started to turn her head. The point of her horn almost poked Cimarrón's eye out, and the horse shied to one side, carrying Hayward too far away.

"You have to strike before she turns," Corado called. "That horn will make your horse shy every time. Try the mulberry heifer on your left."

Hayward reined Cimarrón toward the heifer, moving a little faster, quartering in so his knee did not touch her till he was ready to strike. When he came against her, she bawled and started to run, but he leaned out of the saddle and drove the knife home. The heifer reared up, bawling,

160

and then fell to the ground. She lay there thrashing, and Corado had to run his black in and swing off. He ran around till he could get an opening, then lunged in and struck again. The heifer stiffened in one last spasm, then fell back, motionless. Corado stepped back to his horse, panting.

"You got her on the side. It has to be right on top, right at the pool, between those bones. Try again, now. You have to learn before they start running."

Hayward tried again, on a nervous black bull. This time he dropped the beast with the first stroke. The animals falling on every side and the growing stench of gore in the air were now alarming the herd.

Corado went after a red steer. He spurred his black alongside the beast, sidestepped in, struck, sidestepped out. The steer fell without a sound. It was all very neat, like the intricate steps of a dance. Then Hayward went after one and found out how deceptive that neatness was.

The steer started running, and he spurred Cimarrón after it. His knee bounced against a sweaty shoulder. He saw the steer start to swing its head. He struck. The steer went down, but it fell right into him. He tried to rein aside, but his reactions were too slow. The steer fell heavily against the buckskin, and the horse stumbled, pitching Hayward. He rolled desperately to get out from beneath the falling steer. Corado came on the run through the dust, reined his horse to a dancing halt.

"Isn't so easy as it looks, is it?" he laughed. "Get aboard and try again, Juanito. You'll make a *nuqueador* yet."

Corado caught the buckskin, and Hayward mounted again. He was surrounded by the phantom figures of steers and riders racing back and forth through the yellow haze of dust. The cattle were growing more and more frantic, bolt-

161

ing in all directions. The frenzy seemed to extend to the horsemen. With that same display of barbarism they had shown at the bull and bear fight, they were riding like crazy men, running their horses headlong after steers, taking foolhardy chances and showing off for each other, whooping like wild Indians.

Hayward saw Corado chase after two bulls, running his horse right in between them. He struck to the right, then the left, felling both animals.

"How do you like that, Tico?" he bawled. "Who is the best *nuqueador* now? Can anybody in all the world match Miguel Corado?"

"Try to match this one!" Tico shouted.

He looked around till he saw a steer charging out of the smoke dust. He wheeled his horse and ran it head on at the steer. In the last instant, when it seemed inevitable that the horse and steer should crash headlong, Tico reined aside. As the steer raced past him, so close its horn ripped at his jacket, he struck. The steer bellowed and went down.

"You think that's something?" shouted Corado. "It is nothing. I'll show you real *nuqueo* now. I'll show you *nuqueo* you'll never forget."

Through the haze of dust, Hayward could see that the man's face was flushed, his eyes were glittering. It was as if the excitement of shouting men and bawling steers and pounding hoofs had brought out all his brutal wildness, had filled him with a primitive blood lust. He circled his horse till he sighted a pair of steers. He picked them up and herded them toward a bunch of cattle milling farther off. Every few seconds, the yelling riders would run back in for another kill, and the steer they picked would break from the bunch and make a run for it. Hayward saw Gregorio go after a black bull, and it broke from the main bunch and headed toward Corado. Then Corado whooped in behind the two steers he had been herding. They parted to let his black horse in between them. Gregorio had not caught his black steer, and it was racing blindly toward Corado and the two other steers. Gregorio saw it and pulled up, yelling at Corado.

"Turn them or something! You'll be caught in between. You can't get out if they meet, Corado."

But Corado made no effort to turn his steers aside. Racing between them, his face twisted in a frenzied grin, he ran headlong at Gregorio's bull. Hayward realized what the man intended. He would race toward the bull between his steers until they were only a few paces apart. Then he would drop the steers on either side of him, counting on one of them falling outward so he could veer aside and drop the bull as it charged past. But it was a crazy chance to take. If both steers fell inward, Corado would be pinned between them, and the bull would crash headlong into him, sending him to the ground beneath a ton of thrashing beef.

Hayward saw that Gregorio had stopped his horse dead, and all the other riders within view had pulled their horses down to watch. Yelling like a fiend, spurring his black till its flanks were red with blood, Corado raced headlong between those steers toward the bull.

"Corado!" Hayward shouted desperately. "Now! Now!"

But the man couldn't hear him. The ground trembled to the thunder of hoofs, and the charging bodies were almost lost in the smoke of dust. In the last instant, when it seemed that all four animals were doomed to crash head on, Corado struck. Right and left his body whipped, driving the knife first into the steer on one side, then into the beast on the other. For a moment, Hayward thought Corado was lost. It looked as if both animals would fall inward. Then

163

the one on the right stumbled and spilled outward, allowing Corado to veer the black aside in the last possible moment.

As the bull ran past him, he dodged the horn, then leaned in and struck. It dropped with a bellow. Corado was already twenty feet beyond. He whirled his black and brought it to a snorting, pawing stop. The bull and both steers lay so close together the spot could have been encircled by a ten-foot loop.

"Now," bawled Corado. "Who is the best *nuqueador* in the world?"

None of them answered. They sat their horses in dead silence, amid the bawling of steers and the thunder of hoofs, staring at the three dead beasts lying so close together. But their silence was more eloquent than any cheers could have been.

As if unable to contain the excitement any longer, Corado wheeled his black with a yell and ran back into the scattering herd, striking right and left, whooping crazily. Hayward went back to the work again, lining out after a hairy red steer that was trying to escape. He made dozens of passes, completed less than half of them, had to dismount more than once to finish the job he had botched. It made him appreciate even more Corado's consummate skill. Just trying to kill one steer on the run was lethal enough. The slightest miscalculation could mean a horn in your belly or a thousand pounds of beef and bone crashing down on you.

In an hour, Hayward was so exhausted he had to pull out and rest. The killing was scattered all over the plain now, and some of the riders were even chasing cattle into the sea. A swarm of Indian skinners had taken over, expertly ripping hides off the fallen steers in areas where no rider was working. As soon as the skinners left, the meat

164

cutters took over, butchering the carcasses for jerky and salt beef. After them, the Indian women hauled up green hides, on which they piled the tallow and fat. The hides were folded over and tied and skidded to the try-out grounds. Here, Hayward saw them dumping the tallow and fat into great kettles that smoked over crackling fires.

He watered his horse and went back to work. By dusk it was finished, and only the skinners and butchers and teams of Indian women were left on the field, still working over the carcasses. The men rode down to the sea to wash. They were caked with gore and dust, and they stripped naked for the swim.

Corado looked like a dripping ape emerging from the breakers. He was short-legged, long-armed, completely covered with thick black hair. Beneath its bristly tufts, the muscles lay thickly quilted across his chest and shoulders, bunching and knotting with his slightest movement.

He saw Hayward watching him and emitted his roguish laugh. "How you like that, Juanito? Three steers at once. Is there anybody in the world better than Miguel Corado?"

"Not even when it comes to bragging. I'd just hate to be the steer on the other end of your knife."

"You think that's funny? Sometimes men do *nuqueo*. It's a duel like you never saw."

"I'll stick with the cattle," Hayward said, grinning.

"You better. Now let's go and get some rest. It's going to be a big day again tomorrow."

Hayward sought Aline again, but got no chance to speak with her alone. She was laboring at the trying vats with the Indian women, and there was always someone too near. He went back to the cook fires, ate dinner with the crew, then rolled in to sleep like a dead man from the arduous labors of the day.

165

Chapter Fifteen

By morning another pair of crews had driven cattle in. One of them was made up of Pío Tico and Nicolás. They said El Sombrío had been with them, but they had split up to chase some cattle and had lost him. Hayward saw that this put a distinct tension into the men, and knew they were thinking of the *fantasmas*.

It angered Corado. He put Hayward in El Sombrío's place, sending him out with Pío Tico and Nicolás for more cattle. It was a chance Hayward welcomed. El Sombrío's absence stuck in his mind. The men connected it with the *fantasmas*. Why not? Antonio had run into something up there in the mountains. Could El Sombrío have met the same thing? It was a possibility Hayward could not afford to overlook. Time was running out, and he had to follow any lead, no matter how thin or crazy.

They passed Monterey sometime in the afternoon, pushing their horses hard, and climbed into the Santa Lucias. They reached the Carmel River, and Nicolás told Hayward it was here that El Sombrío had left them.

They flushed a bunch of blackhorns by the river and cut out the brands that didn't belong to the Rancho del Sur. That left them with a dozen head. Nicolás drove the cattle while Hayward and Tico scouted ahead. They rode upriver, and Hayward recognized the landmarks. They were not far from the Gilroy mill. Then they flushed another bunch of cattle and got separated in the chase. Hayward took the chance to head toward the mill. He knew it would not look too suspicious to Tico and Nicolás. It was easy enough for a stranger to lose his way in these mountains.

It was near dusk when he came upon the Gilroy place. Stock were browsing peacefully in the corral, but nobody was in the house. He rode to the mill and saw Dan Gilroy stacking sacks of grain outside the tall building. The man wiped sweat from the grooves of his ruddy face, greeting him.

"Have you been out at all today?" Hayward asked in English.

"Rode a couple of miles back into the hills after a horse that strayed. Why?"

"I thought you might have run across one of our men. El Sombrío didn't come back with the rest of his crew last night."

Gilroy chuckled heartily. "You come to the right place. He always looks me up when he wants a place to sleep off one of his jags. He come in this afternoon, red-eyed and roaring. Sleeping it off inside. Where he gets so much liquor in these mountains, I'll never know."

He went back to work while Hayward entered the dusky mill, with the creak and groan of the wheel drowning all other sounds. He found El Sombrío asleep on a pile of sacks and shook him awake. The man blinked stupidly at him, his eyes filmed and bloodshot. A foolish grin made a quarter moon of his mouth. Hayward could see that he was not yet completely sober.

"You look like you've been on a two-day drunk," Hayward said in Spanish.

"Sure," El Sombrío replied thickly. "Old Don Inocencio made the best wine in California."

Don Inocencio? That rang a bell in Hayward's mind. Beside El Sombrío was the gum-sealed, rawhide bladder these men used for a canteen. Hayward stooped to smell it,

167

grimacing at the reek of the wine. El Sombrío giggled tipsily.

"It's empty. I drank it all."

"How could you be drinking Higuera wine? The old man died years ago, didn't he?"

El Sombrío nodded sagely. "There is enough wine to last my lifetime. But if I told, the whole crew would be up there, and it would be gone in a night."

Hayward was exasperated. So much was still unanswered about the Higuera house. All the trouble he'd run into seemed to center around it — Bardine and Morgan and Antonio.

"Listen, Gloomy One, if you know something about that house that we don't, you've got to tell us."

El Sombrío blinked at him. "Why?"

Hayward knew suddenly that this was one of those crazy leads he could not turn down. There was a key to every puzzle, and he'd run across them in crazier ways than this. He couldn't afford to overlook it. And he knew the only way he could get it was with a lie. He bent toward the man, his face tense.

"Because Carlota has disappeared, you old fool. We are all out hunting her. Do you remember what happened to Don Antonio? Do you remember where it happened? Do you want that to happen to Carlota?"

The old man's face turned white as parchment. He seemed to have trouble breathing. Then he tried to get up. Hayward had to help him.

He said: "How could my little secret have any bearing?"

"Who knows?" Hayward said. "When you're desperate, you've got to try everything."

"Very well, Juanito," El Sombrío said. "I will show you."

They rode southward from the river, crossing Higuera

Cañon five miles inland from the sea. On their right flank now, between them and the ocean, rose the mesa upon which the original Higuera house stood. Its escarpment rose several hundred feet high, so sheer and rocky that even a man on foot could not scale it. It was broken intermittently by narrow cañons that ran back a quarter mile or a half mile, only to reach a dead end. And into one of these cañons El Sombrío finally led Hayward.

The sun died, and the cañon was swallowed in shadow. A wind sprang up, whistling eerily against the rocks. El Sombrío was stone sober now, grimacing with the taste of a hangover in his mouth. They met timber, a feathery mass of cedars and scrub oak, and ran into underbrush beyond. They found a bench that rose halfway up the steep side of the cañon. Riding on this, they finally reached the box end, rising to unscalable heights on every side. El Sombrío dismounted and shoved his way through a matted growth of madroña and stunted cedar. Hayward followed and found the old man standing in the mouth of a tunnel that had been hidden by the brush.

"This is part of the old Higuera winery, Juanito. I knew of it from the old days. It is much easier to reach this entrance than to go around and up the ocean trail. Higuera had Indian labor to cut the tunnels right out of the stone, and in there the wine was aged. Some of the casks are still there. You should see them. A hundred gallons. Five hundred."

"Would these tunnels run underneath the house?"

"Sure. The entrance was right inside the house. But a lot of it crumbled away."

A thin excitement ran through Hayward. He knew he was grasping at straws, but he had to see. He went back to get the pistol out of his saddlebags. It was the one Carlota had given him when they had found Antonio, and Corado had allowed him to keep it on the roundup.

"Let's go in," he said.

He saw the questions fill El Sombrío's face, the doubts, the fears. Then, without a word, the old man turned and hunted around in the mouth of the tunnel till he found a torch he had apparently used before. It was a short length of chaparral, greased with tallow, burned black at one end. They lit it, and Hayward held it, leading El Sombrío. The light flared like a yellow bloom against the stone walls. They soon came to the first cask, black with age. The bung starter El Sombrío had turned was still dripping wine. They passed it, reached a lateral tunnel, and halted. Hayward could hear only the spitting of the torch echoing farther down in the darkness.

They turned into the lateral tunnel. It was blackened in some places, as if the solid rock had been blasted out by gunpowder, and smooth in others, as if from the time-consuming chipping of Indian laborers. Hayward did not know how much farther they went before the murmuring started. It was like the gurgle of far-off water.

Hayward glanced at El Sombrío and saw the primitive fears shining in the old man's eyes.

"You can go back," he said.

El Sombrío moistened his lips. "I am with you, my friend."

Hayward ground the light out against the floor, leaving them in utter darkness. They moved down the tunnel toward the sound, rounding several turns, forced to choose between lateral tunnels. Then the faintest glimmer of light reached them. With El Sombrío hanging like a child to his clothes, Hayward moved on till he reached a corner. From here the sound became recognizable. It was voices.

Hayward could barely see the tunnel now, extending for fifty feet ahead, coming to an abrupt end against a rock wall, with a labyrinth of cross tunnels opening onto it at intervals. He moved down toward the wall, realizing at last that it was an elbow turn. Carefully he and El Sombrío moved to the turn, peered around the corner. They were looking down another short length of tunnel into one end of a big cellar-like room, pierced by the mouths of half a dozen other tunnels. He could see a heap of blankets, a tattered bearskin, a torch bracketed onto the wall, but none of the men. Touching El Sombrío to indicate that he should stay at the corner, Hayward inched around the turn, straining to make out the voices. The acoustics of the hollow place made them unrecognizable, but he could distinguish words now.

"You keep winning like that and you'll have my pants," a man said.

"It's the wine," another grumbled. "You got to quit drinking. He'll catch you napping someday, if you don't."

Hayward checked himself as he heard movement. There was the scrape of a chair. Someone grunted. Then he heard the sound of feet against the rocky floor, moving toward this end of the room.

Panic gripped Hayward. It took a distinct effort not to wheel and seek the safety of the turn. But he realized that the spot where he stood was dark as compared with the room, and he would remain unseen by anyone out there if he did not move. He saw the man's immense shadow thrown against the wall by the torchlight.

Then the man himself appeared. It was James Morgan.

He shambled to one of the wine casks racked at the end of the room, holding a tin cup beneath the bung starter. The yellow light played greasily across his filthy elkhide leggings, pooling black shadows in the hollows beneath his cheekbones. He filled the cup and was turning when a sharp clattering sound came from behind Hayward. In thoughtless reaction, Hayward's head snapped around. He had an instantaneous glimpse of El Sombrío. The old man had started to come around the corner and had brushed against loose shale on the wall, knocking it off.

Hayward whirled back. But already Morgan was reacting. He wheeled halfway around, arm sweeping out. Hayward jerked his pistol up, thinking the man was going to throw the hatchet at his belt. But Morgan snatched a torch from the bracket behind him and threw it. Hayward could not stop his reactions, and was already squeezing the trigger.

But the thrown torch completely blinded him. He jumped back to escape its blazing passage, and it fell at his feet. Then he saw that his shot had missed Morgan. The man still stood in the room, bent forward, staring blankly at Hayward, who was completely illumined by the torch at his feet.

"Larkin!" Morgan roared. "Frenchy . . . Larios! It's Hayward. Get around behind him, cut him off."

Even as he shouted, Morgan pulled his hatchet and started toward Hayward. El Sombrío had regained his feet and was running toward Hayward from behind, shouting: "Juanito, they're coming in from all sides!"

Hayward heard the hollow echo of their running feet in the other tunnels. He backed away from the torch, trying to reload the gun. But Morgan wouldn't give him time. He dragged himself past the sputtering torch, hatchet held out wide. The light came up and flickered across his sweating face. His grin was ugly.

"I told you there'd be other times," he said.

Hayward stopped, clubbing the gun. The echo of those

172

running feet was swelling, and he knew he had to meet Morgan fast, or be completely overpowered. The man slowed down as Hayward stopped and began to shift from side to side, maneuvering for an opening. With a sudden shout, Morgan whipped the hatchet back to throw it. Hayward saw the bright flash of the blade and tried to duck aside. For just that minute he was off balance, and Morgan rushed him instead.

Realizing that it had been a feint, realizing the man had not thrown the hatchet, Hayward tried to recover himself. But Morgan was able to drag himself to reach him while he was still twisted aside. He was bringing the hatchet down at Hayward.

Hayward had only the heavy pistol, and he threw it up wildly. The hatchet struck the brass mounting with a shivering clang. It numbed Hayward's hand, but it deflected the blade. He saw the hatchet swing on down with the impetus of the blow, then saw Morgan catch himself and bring the weapon back in a wicked return swipe.

Hayward wheeled around violently, his back going flat against the wall. The hatchet missed his face by an inch and buried itself in the limestone. The force of the blow had spun Morgan against Hayward, pinning him to the wall. Hayward heard the man grunt, jerking the blade out. Before Morgan could strike again, Hayward brought the heavy pistol up in a sideswiping blow that whipped it viciously across Morgan's face. The gun came apart with the force of the blow, and Morgan staggered backward with a broken cry.

Hayward lunged after him. His plunging weight carried Morgan across the tunnel and against the opposite wall. Before the man could recover, Hayward dropped his broken pistol and caught Morgan's long black hair in both hands,

173

smashing the man's head against the stone wall, hearing the shouts of battle from behind. This time Morgan went completely limp and crumpled against the wall.

Gasping for air, Hayward wheeled to see El Sombrío and a black-faced *californio* rolling back and forth on the floor, locked in deadly combat. It all happened in a single instant after that, so fast that Hayward didn't even have time to start toward them before it was over.

Even as Hayward wheeled, he saw El Sombrío knee the other man in the groin. The *californio* doubled over, losing his grip on El Sombrío's knife wrist, and the old man plunged the blade deep. At the same time, the clatter of feet in the cross tunnels made a great echo all through the place. El Sombrío rolled the *californio*'s body off him and scrambled to his feet just in time to meet a black-bearded Frenchman who burst from the mouth of a right-hand tunnel. El Sombrío lunged at the man with his knife. The Frenchman fired his pistol, still running forward. El Sombrío jerked with the bullet, but his impetus carried him into the man, the knife going hilt deep in the Frenchman's belly.

Even as they fell, Hayward heard another man running into the main tunnel from the other side. In desperation, he lunged for the hatchet Morgan had dropped, scooping it off the floor as another buckskinned trapper burst into the open. Hayward heaved the hatchet as the man jerked his pistol up to fire. The hatchet buried itself in the trapper's chest, and the shot went wild, ricocheting off the stone walls with a piercing scream. The man fell back with blood spouting like a fountain from his chest.

Hayward stood blankly for a moment, swaying on widespread feet, so drained by the savage violence of it that his mind would hold no thought for a moment. Then he stumbled to El Sombrío, dropping to a knee beside him. It took but a glance to see that the old man was dead.

A man couldn't afford much sentiment in a job like this, but for a moment a savage grief ran through Hayward and made him sick. It was an effort to tear his attention away from the old man. The tunnel was deathly silent. Out in the big room the only sound was the spitting of the torches. Hayward pulled the Frenchman's big Cherington pistol from beneath his body and found some powder and lead on the man and carefully reloaded the piece. Still there was no sound from within the room.

He got to his feet then and cautiously made his way toward the big chamber. He stopped at the mouth of the tunnel, flattened against the wall. He could not even hear breathing. Then, suddenly, chains clanked. Hayward took his chance.

"Bardine?"

"Over here," a man answered. "It's all right. There's nobody else in the room."

Hayward stepped into the chamber. He saw a table of whipsawed lumber and half a dozen chairs in its center. Beyond that, on one of the rude bunks built against the wall, his hands and feet shackled to a stout chair with short chains, sat Roger Bardine.

The resemblance to Aline was strong. There was the same peasant strength to his black-eyed, blunt-featured face, the same earthy vitality to his stocky, solid-muscled body. His hair was a grizzled iron gray, matted over his ears and at the base of his neck. He had a gray-tinged beard that needed barbering just as badly, curling against a blue military coat with one button missing.

Moving into the room, Hayward said: "I guess I've got that missing button."

The man stared blankly at him. "It was you that night,

175

down at the other building?"

"I'm John Hayward, the agent Washington sent to get you out of here. Are we through, now?"

"Nobody else upstairs," Bardine said. "Why don't you sit down a minute? You look as if it went pretty rough back in the tunnel."

Hayward realized he was trembling in reaction to all the violence now. The letdown was borne against him suddenly, like an unbearable weight, and he sagged into a chair at the table.

"Not that, so much," he said. "A man just got killed back there. A good man."

"I'm sorry," Bardine said.

Hayward stared blankly at the floor for a moment, feeling a bitter self-recrimination for bringing El Sombrío into this. Then he gathered himself, waving the pistol at the shackles. Bardine told him the key was in Morgan's pocket, and he went back to get it. He kept himself from looking at El Sombrío, feeling the sickness well up to gag him again, and took the key in to free Bardine.

"How about filling in the blank spots now?" he said. "They originally held you in the second Higuera place, down in the cañon?"

"That's right," Bardine said. "That's why Larios shot at you when you were chasing those mustangs. It looked as if you were going to drive the horses right down Higuera Cañon to the spot where they were holding me. When he hit Antonio Mateo, Larios thought he'd stopped you. But when you came to the buildings down in the cañon and almost got me, they moved me up here for safekeeping."

"How did Antonio get murdered?" Hayward asked.

"They were afraid he knew the leader of the *fantasmas*, as his father had. They'd already made several attempts to

176

kill Antonio. He practically walked into their hands that night."

"He'd been drinking," Hayward said. "He must have sought refuge up here with some crazy idea that the *fantasmas* were chasing him. He and Carlota had played here as kids, I guess. He always said they'd get him when he was drunk."

"They hadn't had time to dispose of Antonio's body when you showed up," Bardine explained. "Morgan attacked you that night because he was afraid you'd find the entrance to this winery, if you kept looking."

"And these are the *fantasmas en la noche?*"

"Yes," Bardine said. "They didn't call themselves that. It came from the people." He smiled ruefully. "Latins do have a penchant for grandiloquent names, don't they?"

"But this is no comic opera."

"No, Hayward." Bardine's face darkened. "This is deadly serious. We've always had political strife in California. The country's passed back and forth through the hands of a dozen different factions. But never anything as deadly as this. A power-crazed man at the head of a band of cut-throats who are growing so large and so well organized that they stand a good chance of taking over all of California, if they aren't stopped. The only faction they really fear is the Americans. We've grown pretty strong here in the last years and might break it up, if we stand together. Captain Sloat is off Central America with a couple of warships, and Frémont is in the Sierras with a detachment of the Army. The *fantasmas* took me hostage with the idea of preventing those forces from joining. They planned to threaten to kill me, if Sloat were to come up here and put a single American sailor ashore, or if Frémont interfered. I told them they were crazy to think that would stop Sloat or Frémont."

"Not so crazy," Hayward said. "After all, we have no official right to interfere in this. The whole situation would be mighty ticklish, and the threat of your death would probably be just the thing to keep Sloat and Frémont from action. But why did the *fantasmas* jump you so quickly? Why arouse this suspicion by capturing you before they were ready to strike?"

"I forced their hand. They'd meant to take me hostage the day they struck, but I found out who their leader was. Old Don Fernando Mateo told me the very day he was killed on that bear hunt."

"Is it Rodríguez?"

"No," Bardine said. "*Alcalde* Rodríguez plays both end against the middle from every direction. I think he actually believes the *fantasmas* are a bunch of Americans trying to depose him here. That's why he closed the port to us. But he's also willing to make a deal with the *fantasmas* if he believes it would be to his advantage. That's why he wouldn't do anything to Morgan when Morgan showed up in the Pacific House on the day of the bull and bear fight. Morgan told me about that."

"If Rodríguez isn't the leader, who is?"

"Miguel Corado."

Chapter Sixteen

James Morgan was dead for sure this time, and all the others. They didn't even have time to bury El Sombrío, much less take him back. More *fantasmas* were likely to show up at any time, Bardine said, and the quicker they got out, the better. With a deep reluctance, Hayward left El Sombrío there, knowing his people would take care of him when he was discovered, and led Bardine out the tunnel to the pair of horses by its mouth. There they headed for Monterey Bay.

And all the way, Hayward was thinking about Corado.

Bardine saw it, and finally spoke. "You find it hard to accept?"

Hayward nodded. "I had no idea, no inkling."

"He kept his activities amazingly secret. Part of it lay in the fact that he wouldn't let a man join till he was perfectly sure of him. Only a few trusted ones on the Mateo crew even knew. But Corado has gathered a powerful force, Hayward, a force that might well take over this section of California."

Hayward said: "You know what *compadre* means . . . in Spanish?"

"Corado told me about that, too," Bardine said. "He told me all his life he had been looking for a *compadre* like you. He said you would conquer California together. I thought at first you were one of those white renegades he'd picked up, like James Morgan. Then I heard you came off the *Noah*, and figured it out. You played it well."

"It ceased to be an act, Bardine. I had really come to

179

consider Corado my *compadre*."

"Then I'm sorry for you. I guess I understand. Corado could be a rare friend, under other circumstances. He's pretty brutal and primitive, but you won't meet another man like him in a lifetime. But this thing has warped him, Hayward. He won't do the peons any good, if he gets in power. He's merely using their cause as an excuse to gain his own ends. Rodríguez's rule here has really not been bad. His few transgressions will seem saintly beside what you'll have under a man like Corado. It will be a tyranny, a rule of violence and bloodshed."

"But why? Does Corado want power that badly?"

"I suppose it had a legitimate start. He's mostly Indian, you know, and his parents were killed in a fight with some big landholders. It made him bitter, and he vowed vengeance. But I have the feeling it's something more than that, something deeper, something that's eaten at him, corroded him, till he's completely warped."

"What could it be?"

"That's it. I only had glimpses of it. I couldn't quite identify it. He never spoke of it, but there's something more driving him, Hayward."

They pushed hard after that, passing Monterey while it was yet night, reaching the slaughtering grounds before the darkness had lifted. Hayward left Bardine in the willows by the creek and went in to find Aline. He awoke her gently, a hand over her mouth to keep her from crying out. She was sleeping in her clothes and crawled from the blankets, following him out of camp.

"Tico and Nicolás came in earlier," she said. "They told us they had lost you in the mountains. There was much talk of the *fantasmas,* and some of the men were on the verge of deserting. It made Miguel mad. He took Tico and

180

went to find you and El Sombrío himself."

Hayward led her to the creek, and, when she saw her father, she could hardly contain herself. The joy of their reunion was a good thing to see. Bardine held Aline tightly while she sobbed and laughed against his chest. He patted her, smiling past her head at Hayward.

"She is a strange one, Hayward, a wild one. But she is all I have." Then he pulled her gently free. "We have no time to talk. Captain Lansing came here for more than hides. He has orders to take us aboard the *Noah* till this trouble is over."

They went to the deserted beach, where the hides lay in piles, awaiting the ship's boats. Hayward built a fire and used a hide to make the signals he and Lansing had agreed upon, smothering the fire four times, letting it flare up again. Aline huddled against her father in the chill wind, too joyful at his return to question him. Soon the ship's longboat came booming in on a breaker, and half a dozen barefooted seamen leaped out in the surf to haul it ashore. The bosun jumped from the stern, running up to pump Hayward's hand.

"I never thought I'd see you again, Hayward, I admit I never did. Is this what you came for?"

"You won't have to read it in the Boston papers, Bo," Hayward said with a grin. "Meet Roger Bardine, United States consul, late prisoner of the phantoms in the night."

Somebody kept the binnacle light blinking to guide them back to the ship, but once they were aboard even that was doused. The bosun led them to the captain's quarters. Here, with all ports shrouded, Lansing greeted them.

"This is an occasion," he said. "I must admit I returned with very little hope of seeing you."

"You underestimated Hayward, then," Bardine said.

181

Lansing turned his narrow Yankee face to Hayward. "I must admit I did. My apologies, Mister Hayward."

"Not necessary. You were right, Captain Lansing. It was nothing to laugh at. There's something ugly brewing in this country. Something that stands to wipe out a whole way of life, if it isn't stopped. And it's too good a way of life to lose."

Lansing frowned. "You've changed. When I put you ashore, it was just another job, just another place. All you hoped was that they'd have a couple of pretty wenches to keep it lively while you were there."

"Maybe I have changed," Hayward admitted.

"What is it that threatens the country?"

"A revolution," Bardine said. "Led by a man who is using it to avenge his own personal wrongs, a *mestizo* named Corado, with the power to take over, if he gets a few breaks."

They heard Aline draw a sharp breath, and turned to her. She was staring wide-eyed at her father. "Miguel?" she said. "You can't be right, Father."

Bardine frowned at her. "I saw him, Aline. A dozen times."

"But it can't be," she said. "Not Miguel. He couldn't do this killing, these cruelties. . . ."

"He's capable of anything under the sun, my dear."

"Then it's a good thing we got you out when we did," Lansing said. "My orders are to put back to Washington as soon as you're aboard."

Bardine gaped at him. "We can't do that. We've got to stay and do what we can for these people."

"It's a foreign country," Lansing said. "We have no official right to interfere. We haven't enough men to do any good, anyway. All I can do is take aboard the American citizens that want the safety of the boat. I'd lose my commission, if I went any further. And all you'd do is lose your head, if you went back. You've got your duty, the same as I have, Bardine. You're the only one who has a true picture of what's going on here. Washington needs that information in the worst way."

"He's right," Hayward told Bardine. "You're more valuable to all concerned aboard this ship. But you can put me back on the beach, Captain Lansing. Somebody's got to warn these people. We can't just stand aside and let their lives be torn apart."

"You'd be signing your own death warrant by going back," Bardine said. "As soon as Corado finds I'm gone, he'll know he has to strike. Colonel Archuleta hasn't got enough troops in town to stand off a gang of untold renegades. Corado will be in command of Monterey within an hour after he gets there."

Hayward shook his head stubbornly. "I've got to do it."

Lansing exploded: "Are you completely insane?"

Bardine was studying Hayward shrewdly. "I think the country's got under his skin, Captain. It does that to some men. No other place will ever satisfy them, once they've learned to love this one."

Hayward realized the man was right. He had never known a land where laughter came so easily, where nature was so bountiful, where people knew how to live so fully and joyfully. He was remembering the countless hours in the corral, learning a way of riding more magnificent than he had ever known before. Remembering the whoops of the *vaqueros* as they swept through the corrals, roping at everything in sight and yelling like a bunch of children at play. Remembering El Sombrío.

He felt a bitter need to avenge the old man. How El Sombrío had loved this land, despite his constant grumbling!

Hayward recalled the simple peace of sitting beside the old man, their backs to some sun-baked wall, staring out across the grain turned to a yellow sea by the sun, thinking that a man could very happily spend the rest of his life in this golden, indolent country. There were others who loved it the same way. And how many of them would lose it — as El Sombrío had lost it — if Corado were not stopped?

But there was more than the land, more than El Sombrío. There was Carlota. There was the first time he had kissed her, when it was a joke, and the last time, when it was profoundly serious. There was the brooding passion of her that struck a corresponding passion in him, and the pride that he hated so and loved so all at once. He saw it fully now, something that had been working at him so long. There had been a dozen lands, and now there was only one. There had been a hundred girls, and now there was only one.

"You'd better put me ashore, Captain Lansing."

"I'll go with him," Aline said.

"I want no more of this foolishness," Lansing said. "There will be no going ashore for either of you."

Something flashed through Aline's eyes, that hint of wildness Hayward had seen when Corado cast her aside. Then, without warning, she wheeled and rushed up the companionway. Her father lunged after her, calling sharply, but she beat him to the door and plunged out. They all reached the deck in time to see her at the rail, climbing on top, jumping. Hayward heard the splash below, ran to the rail, and looked off into the pitch blackness.

"Clark!" shouted Lansing. "Bring a lantern. Bosun, get a crew into that longboat."

Hayward knew what was in Aline's mind now, and knew how woefully late the men in the boat would be. He climbed atop the rail himself and dropped off. The water chilled him, but he came sputtering to the surface and struck out. He was only half a minute behind the girl, but could see nothing in the darkness. He stopped to listen and could only hear the shout of the bosun, the creak of oars. He struck out the other way.

The boat joined him in the search, the lantern shedding its feeble light on the water. They even circled the brig to see if she had gone on that side to throw them off. Finally, after a futile half hour, they gave up. Hayward took the Jacob's ladder back aboard and shed his dripping clothes. The bosun got him a wool sweater and a pair of duck pants.

"It's no wonder you couldn't find her," Bardine said. "She swims like a fish. I wonder what got into her head. She's always been such a wild one. I never could control her, much as I love her. We can't leave now, Captain."

Lansing shook his head disgustedly. "I'll lay off the point here till we see if she can be found."

"You'll have to send someone ashore, then," Hayward said.

Lansing frowned, considering it. Hayward was thinking of Aline. He knew well enough, now, why she had gone. He was remembering that strange, wide-eyed expression she always got with Corado. Hayward hadn't thought about it at the time. He'd been too busy trying to figure out how far he could trust her. But now he knew.

"All right," Lansing said. "You can go. As long as Bardine and his daughter are the only ones who know your true identity, you'll be comparatively safe."

Hayward grinned. "I don't know about that. Don't you really know why she went back?"

"How could I?" asked the captain.

"She's in love with Corado."

Chapter Seventeen

It was daylight when Hayward got ashore. Already the teams of Indians were dragging stacks of hides to the beach. The riders were gathering out on the flats to slaughter the steers the crews had brought in. It made Hayward realize how treacherous the problem of warning them was. Which were *fantasmas,* which were not? If Corado was the leader, could any man in the Mateo crew be trusted? Some did not know the truth, and were loyal to the Mateos. But Hayward had no way of knowing which ones. So he avoided the men, reached the horse lines by a circuitous route, saddled his buckskin, and turned it south toward Monterey. Colonel Archuleta was the most logical one to warn, and Hayward knew he could, at least, trust him.

He pushed the horse hard, and it was still early morning when he reached Monterey. There was a strange tension in the town. Knots of men were gathered before the saloons, the taverns, even some of the houses, talking among themselves. Hayward pulled up within sight of the plaza, seeing a half dozen dust-coated riders enter town from the south along the Camino Real. They rode down to the custom house and dismounted, joining a group in the shade of the balcony.

Another cavalcade came in along the Santa Cruz road. They watched Hayward closely as they passed, but he recognized none of them. They were black-faced men in tattered rawhides and worn serapes, filmed yellow with dust, faces hollowed with the fatigue of a long hard ride. They passed across the plaza and pulled up at the bull and bear pit near *Alcalde* Rodríguez's house. Hayward followed them, puzzled.

There was a group of soldiers lounging before the long barracks fronting on the plaza. Hayward recognized the corporal who had first escorted him to the *alcalde*'s house, and checked his horse by the man.

"Where's everybody coming from? Are you going to have a bull and bear fight or something?"

The corporal shook his head. "I don't know, *señor*. It has been this way all morning. Something is afoot."

Hayward asked after Archuleta, and the corporal said the colonel had not yet arrived. Hayward turned his horse across the Calle Principal and onto the road that led to the Archuleta house, set back in a grove of trees on the hill. There was the usual line of horses, stamping and fretting at a rack down by the peons' quarters back of the big house, but no horses at the rack in front of the main building. He was glad for that. It meant he could see Archuleta alone. He hitched his buckskin at the end of the rack near the patio, so it would not be visible from the road, then walked to the front door and knocked.

It was opened. Pío Tico stood there. He had a pistol, pointed at Hayward's belly.

For a moment, both of them stood without speaking, gripped by the same surprise. Then Tico's eyes glittered in his mahogany-hued face, and he smiled maliciously.

"Come in, *señor*. Come in."

Hayward could see past Tico and into the great room. It was filled with dark-faced men in tattered cotton shirts, greasy rawhide leggings, dusty serapes. Their spurs jingled and rattled constantly with their restless movement. Four or five were seated at a long table, eating and drinking wolfishly. Another group stood near the north end, all

187

watching Hayward, smoking nervously. A pair of them stood beside Colonel Archuleta, who sat in a chair. There was a bloody scratch on his seamed cheek, and his blue coat had been torn. At the other end of the room, in a chair by the fireplace, sat Carlota. Her hair was parted in the middle, drawn severely back to a bun tied at the nape of her neck. Its jet-black color was in startling contrast to the pallor of her face. Her hands were locked in the lap of her blue gown, and she was leaning forward tensely as she stared at Hayward.

And beside her stood Corado.

He had wheeled as Tico opened the door, and now he came toward Hayward eagerly, his spurs clattering like a cavalry charge. "Juanito, you have come. How did you do it? How did you know where to find me?" He reached Tico and elbowed him aside, pushing at the gun. "Do not hold the pistol on my *compadre*, fool. He has come to join us."

He caught Hayward's arm, pulling him in, pounding him on the back. Hayward knew now what had happened. He had known the instant Tico had opened the door. But with Carlota in their midst, he could see only one way to play it. If Corado did not suspect him yet, there was only one way.

"I came to tell Carlota the hide skinning was almost over," he said. "What do you mean . . . join you?" He turned to Archuleta. "What's this all about, Colonel?"

Archuleta's hands knotted about the arms of the chair. "*Señor* Hayward. . . ."

"Never mind," Corado interrupted. "I will tell him." He grasped Hayward by both shoulders. "I would have told you before, Juanito, but I had to be sure. Would you give me your saddle?"

"Of course."

"Your horse?"

188

"Take him."

"Your life?"

"It's yours."

Corado laughed loudly, face flushed like an excited child's. "I knew it!" he said, pounding Hayward on the shoulders. "You are my *compadre*. And if I showed you a new world, where every woman is ours . . . all the liquor . . . all the land . . . would you fight for it with me? Would you conquer it with me?"

Hayward grinned. "We'll be back to back on top of that table."

Corado roared with excitement. "And there isn't anybody in the whole world who can lick us." He wheeled to Carlota. "Did you hear that? I told you he was my *compadre*. I told you he'd ride with me."

Hayward saw a deep disappointment settle into Carlota's white face. She stared at him unbelievingly. It was an effort to keep his grin. Corado was clapping him on the shoulder again.

"So now you shall know, Juanito." He waved his hand at the men again. "These are *fantasmas*. I am their leader. We take Monterey today. We take California tomorrow."

He stopped, staring intensely at Hayward to see his reaction. Hayward allowed a proper amount of surprise to widen his eyes. He stared around at the men, at Carlota. Then he grinned again.

"It's about time somebody dumped Rodríguez off that fat seat of his."

Corado pounded him again, whooping with delight. "I knew that's the way you felt. Why didn't I tell you a long time ago?" He ran to the window, tearing aside a heavy drape, pointing down through the trees to the town. "Did you see them, Juanito? All over town? They are gathering.

189

From a hundred miles away, they are gathering. Who can stand against us? Fifty soldiers in town. I'll have five hundred men by nightfall. We'll take the town with one blow. Then who will get worked and beaten and whipped and run down in the street as if they were pigs in the mud?" He broke off, peering suspiciously at Hayward. "What are you staring at so strangely? Don't you think I can do it?"

"Give me a little time to get over my surprise, Miguel. Of course, I think you can do it. You're the only man with the strength to hold these people together. Who else could have kept an organization so secret while he built it up? Who could have kept his identity unknown for so long?"

The man's shout was triumphant. "You are right, Juanito! Without me, they could never do this. I will be the king." He turned to Carlota. "And she will be my queen. Will she not make the most beautiful of queens?" He leered at her. "Why do you fight it, Carlota? There is not another in all of California who would not give her soul to occupy the throne with Miguel Corado."

A quick, savage breath swelled the white slopes of her breasts against her square-cut bodice. "You can't be so mad. They'll hang you in the plaza."

He leaned toward her, his voice husky. "I do not think you are worrying about that. You are going back through those days when you whipped me with your quirt, when you insulted me, when you treated me like a child . . . like a dog. You are remembering how I looked at you then. You are thinking of what must have been on my mind. I was waiting, wasn't I? Waiting for this day. And now it has come. And I could have my revenge. I could take a quirt to you! I could even have you pulled apart by horses, or turn you over to these men."

"Corado . . . !"

190

"But you know I won't. You know that isn't the revenge I seek. That wasn't what stayed in my mind, when I was waiting. Because there were good times, too, Carlota. Remember how many fine rides we had together . . . remember how often we laughed together . . . how many horses I gentled and trained for you? And you pleased yourself by thinking it was merely the indulgence of a man who had watched over you since your childhood. But now you know that isn't true. It wasn't revenge I was waiting for, and it wasn't fatherly indulgence I was giving you." He leaned toward her, a heavy-lidded sensuality coming to his eyes. "Now you know what it was, all the time . . . and it shocks you."

"Don't be a fool," she said thinly. "Do you think I am that naïve?"

"Perhaps it disgusts you, then?" he asked softly.

She drew a thin little breath. "Perhaps it does."

"I'm glad if it does," he shouted. "I'm glad it disgusts you, because then I'll have to break you like I'd break a horse, Carlota, and every minute of it will be sweet as honey. When I'm through, you won't be disgusted. You'll know why every wench in California would give her soul for Miguel Corado!"

He was breathing heavily, his face flushed and sweating, a strange glitter in his eyes. And suddenly Hayward had the key to the man's drive, the motive behind it all that Bardine had sensed but had never quite seen. It must be Carlota.

Maybe the roots of Corado's rebellion lay in the killing of his parents, the treatment of his people by Rodríguez and a few others. But these roots had been buried long ago. Hayward remembered now the look of Corado's eyes when they had discussed Carlota.

You don't know how it was, watching Carlota grow up,

191

teaching her how to ride, to shoot. . . .

And now Hayward understood. A lifetime of that. A lifetime of wanting something more than he had ever wanted anything else. Before him every day, maddening him with her pride, her indifference, her anger, or her indulgence, treating him alternately like a fatherly adviser and a child, but never as he wanted her to treat him, never as a man.

Only a person who knew Corado intimately, who had seen his animal depths, his vast capacities, his primitive hungers, his incredible lusts, could understand how such a thing could drive him. But for a person who understood him, it was easy to see how Carlota could become a symbol of all he wanted. Easy to see how that symbol could quickly become the living, burning goal, blotting out all the things that had originally motivated him, until in the end it was the only thing he really sought.

Perhaps Corado was still fooling himself. Perhaps he was still trying to tell himself that he had organized the *fantasmas* to avenge the death of his parents, the wrongs committed against his people by Rodríguez and his kind. But it was only an excuse. He was only using the *fantasmas* for his own warped ends. His own goal had become twisted in his mind, as Bardine had said, eating at him through all those years, corroding him, until domination and possession of this one woman represented the whole cause to him.

Corado became aware of Hayward's attention on him and slowly turned, the flush fading from his face. But before he could speak, a knock shook the main door. A nervous shifting ran through the men. Tico lifted his pistol once more, glancing at Corado, who nodded for him to open the door. They all waited, hands on the butts of their pistols, while Tico swung the door inward.

It was Aline.

Chapter Eighteen

Although Aline's arrival was something Hayward had remotely considered, he still felt the shock of it run sickly through him, now that it had happened. Corado frowned suspiciously at her.

"What the hell are you doing here?"

She came in. Her cheeks were smudged, her skirt soiled with the sweat of a horse. She was looking steadily at Hayward, and her voice sounded strangely brittle.

"I got a horse at the camp," she said. "If you hadn't been on that buckskin, I'd have beaten you."

"Aline!" Corado said sharply.

She turned to him. Her breath made a husky sound in the room. Hayward saw it coming now, and knew he would have only one chance to make his break. His only hope lay in their moment of surprise, when they found out. He realized that the four of them — Tico and Corado and Aline and himself — were all standing in a bunch by the door, near the south end of the room, near Carlota. The other men were all nearer the north end, either bunched by Archuleta or sitting at the table. If Hayward could maneuver so that Corado would stand between him and those men, he would have that instant when they could not fire for fear of hitting their leader. Tico was the only dubious factor. He still had his gun out.

"I thought you'd be here," Aline told Corado. "I didn't know about you and the *fantasmas,* but I knew how you felt about Carlota, and I knew, if the time ever came, you'd be after her."

193

Hayward took a step that put Corado between him and the others.

"She's no good for you, Miguel," Aline went on. "You'll never really have Carlota, no matter what you do. You'll find that out sooner or later. When a woman isn't yours, you can't have her, no matter what you do. I can wait till you find out."

"Aline," Corado said angrily. "What the hell are you talking about?"

She didn't answer him. She turned slowly to Hayward. Her eyes were squinted almost shut, and her voice sounded forced.

"I don't want to do this," she said. "If you go now, if you give me your word you'll leave the country, it will be all right."

Carlota came slowly to her feet, staring at Aline, then at Hayward, trying to identify the strange tension building in the room. Hayward had nothing to say. He took another step that placed him near enough to Tico. The man glanced at him in a puzzled way, but did not raise his gun. A taut plea came into Aline's face.

"Please . . . Hayward."

He shook his head. "You know I can't."

Tears squeezed from her squinted eyes. He saw the struggle run through her till her face looked twisted. Then that anger, that underlying wildness, widened her eyes, making them flash, and she blurted it out.

"All right. You're a fool. I can't help it if you saved my father. I can't let you do this to Miguel."

Corado looked blankly at her. "Saved your father?"

"He isn't your friend, Miguel. He's here to stop you. He's the spy they sent to get my father, and now he'll try to stop you. He'll kill you, if he has to."

Corado wheeled toward Hayward, his face still blank with shock. Tico's lips were parted. But understanding was burgeoning in his eyes, and Hayward knew he would bring that pistol up in another moment. It had to be now.

Hayward lunged into the man, wrenching the weapon from his hand. At the same time he caught him by the belt and swung him around into Corado. They both staggered backward toward the other men. Hayward wheeled and ran for Carlota.

"The hall!" he shouted. "The hall!"

She understood in an instant, and whirled to run for the open hall door directly on her right. He wheeled as he followed her. Both Tico and Corado had recovered. But they still blocked off the other men from firing. A couple of the men were running aside to get a clear shot at Hayward. He jerked his gun up and fired at the first one to appear from behind Corado. The man doubled over, dropping his gun, and pitched forward.

As Hayward reached the door, Corado shoved Tico out of his way and yanked a pistol from his belt. Hayward threw his empty pistol at the man and saw it hit Corado full in the face. Then he was in the hall, slamming the heavy door shut. Gunfire rang out in the other room then. Bullets ate through the wood of the door, kicked adobe from the wall into Hayward's face. One stung his thigh. He ran heavily against Carlota's silken resilience, pushed her hard down the hall.

"Through the patio. My buckskin's near the gate."

They ran down the dark hall, out onto the flagstoned patio. They heard the hall door torn open behind them, heard Corado shouting, the pounding of feet. Hayward and Carlota rushed across the patio, unlatched the door, ran outside. The men's first natural reaction had been to follow

195

them down the hall, only thinking of the front door later. For not until Hayward had mounted the buckskin, swinging Carlota up in front of him, was the front door opened.

Tico was the first one out. He had no gun, and all he could do was shout when he saw them. Hayward wheeled the buckskin and spurred it into the trees. The next man out took a snap shot at them, but it went wild. Then men were streaming from both the patio door and the front door. But Hayward was out of effective range by then. The men had left their horses down by the corrals, apparently to hide them from anyone approaching the house. With futile shouting, they wheeled and ran for them, as Hayward spurred Cimarrón deeper into the grove.

He passed through the trees, slid down a steep bank onto the road. The gunshots had apparently been heard in town. There was already a rattle of firing from the main street.

"The *fantasmas* must think it's the signal," Hayward said. "We've set the whole thing off."

He turned north along the road. He knew he had to get Carlota out of this somehow. The only truly safe place would be the *Noah*, and it was in his mind to take her there. But Corado and his men plunged out of the trees behind them, sliding their horses down the bank onto the road, yelling and shooting. The *fantasmas* that had been bunched at the upper end of the Calle Principal saw this, and immediately guessed what was happening. Half a dozen of them darted across the road, opening fire, blocking Hayward off from the northern route. He had to wheel back, plunging off the road into more scrubby timber.

He came out on a street that ran beneath the old *presidio*, leading to the beach. Corado was still hard on their trail. As they passed a cross street, they could see the battle raging on the main street. A group of men in tattered buckskins were besieging the Pacific Building. Callahan and his servants were on the balcony, putting up a desperate fight, and gunsmoke made a greasy black stain in the air.

The buckskin raced out onto the beach, kicking a scarf of white sand into the air. But there were a dozen *fantasmas* at the custom house, cutting Hayward off from any hope of escape along the beach toward the north. With Corado directly behind, all he could do was wheel the horse south.

Carlota flung a white-faced glance over his shoulder. "You surprised us all," she panted. "Corado didn't even think of you, when he found those dead men in the tunnel up at the Higuera place. He told me about it. He said he and Pío Tico had left the slaughtering to hunt for El Sombrío. When they couldn't find him, they went up to the Higuera place to check on Bardine. When they found Bardine gone, they knew they had to strike before he could warn anyone. They weren't ready, but they had to strike. They thought El Sombrío had led Archuleta there, or maybe Rodríguez, or even the Gilroys. But you didn't even enter Corado's mind. You played your rôle too well for him, Juan."

Hayward didn't answer. Why did they all think it had been a rôle?

A few minutes of hard running took them off the beach and into the rocky crags of Point Pinos. They plunged into a grove of twisted cypresses and could no longer see Corado behind them.

They turned inland once more, with the buckskin picking its way over the treacherous, rocky terrain. Its labored breathing filled the shadowy groves with a husky roar. They left the trees, the crags, saw a curve of hard ground ahead. Then four *fantasmas* burst from a stand of pine farther in-

197

land and wheeled toward them. Hayward realized how he was trapped, now. Corado had fanned them out to cover the whole point and cut him off wherever he turned.

He heard Carlota's helpless sob as he wheeled the buckskin toward the coast. It was the only way he could go. As they pulled up on the rocky headland overlooking the beach, Hayward caught sight of Corado and three *fantasmas* riding the shore farther south. They had bypassed him when he had turned inland, and now they had cut him off from heading farther down the coast. They caught sight of him before he could pull the buckskin back, and wheeled around, returning at a run. He could go no way but back toward town. It was a futile effort. Corado had left men on the beach.

As soon as Hayward appeared in the last rocks overlooking the shore, he saw half a dozen riders fanned out across the white sand. They were competely cut off. Hayward looked back at Corado, followed by three of his men, galloping their horses recklessly across the rocky point behind. There was only one thing left now.

"Do you think the *fantasmas* would stand a chance without Corado?" Hayward asked.

"Of course not," she said. "He's the only one who could hold them together."

Hayward spurred the buckskin down the steep rocks and onto the cove of sheltered sand. He rode the horse right up against the curve of rocks at the southern end of the beach, then stopped. He told Carlota to climb down. Eyes wide, looking at him wonderingly, she complied. He told her to stand right against the rocks and then positioned the buckskin in front of her. Then he took the knife from his leggings.

With a clatter of crumbling shale, Corado pushed his

198

black down off the rocks and onto the beach. He pulled it up there, facing Hayward across a hundred feet of bone-white sand, with his riders plunging down behind and gathering around him. Corado settled into his saddle, staring at Hayward.

"I wish it wasn't this way, Juanito. You were my *compadre*. We could have had a world together."

"And now you've got it," Hayward said. "There isn't another man who could have done it, is there? Drinking or fighting or wenching, not a one who could match you. But how about *nuqueo?*"

"*Nuqueo?*" Corado looked puzzled, but he couldn't help taking the bait. "I am better at that than anything. You saw. Who could match me?"

"I saw you with some steers, Corado. But whoever saw you with a man?"

Corado looked at the knife in Hayward's hand. "Are you crazy, Juanito?"

"If you want Carlota so much, you must be willing to fight for her. You aren't afraid to fight, are you?"

"Juanito . . . !"

"Your men will always wonder, Corado. They know you wouldn't be matched when it comes to drinking or wenching or fighting. But they'll always wonder about *nuqueo*."

The man's face was flushed with anger. "I don't have to prove it. They know nobody can beat me."

"Do they?" Hayward asked. He saw that he was touching Corado's huge, primitive vanity. The man looked from side to side. His men stirred restlessly, their faces black-shadowed beneath their hats, their horses fiddling. It might have meant anything. But Hayward knew how Corado was interpreting it. "They'll always wonder, Corado," he called. "They'll always remember you backed down before the American, when it came to *nuqueo*."

"Damn you!" Corado shouted. "Nobody backed down!"

"Juan!" It was Carlota's voice, sharp with fear.

But Corado had already snatched his knife from his leggings and was spurring his black into a dead run toward Hayward. Hayward touched Cimarrón with his spurs, and the buckskin leaped toward Corado. He saw the man's glittering eyes, his taut face, and knew that his rage blotted out any memory of their past comradeship. But Hayward had his moment of poignant reluctance, when he would have given anything to change it all.

Then everything was swept from his mind but the thunder of hoofs and the whistle of wind and the sight of that black horse racing headlong at him. He was remembering the incredible feat Corado had shown them at the *nuqueo* grounds, and knew he did not have the skill to meet the man head on. When they were five feet apart, he touched Cimarrón's neck with the reins, and the horse shifted leads for a left turn. Corado had been waiting for it and veered his black to meet it. But it had only been a feint. Even as Cimarrón shifted leads, Hayward touched the reins to the other side of his neck.

Few other horses could have shifted back, right in the middle of changing leads that way. But the buckskin did it, veering to the right instead of the left. Corado was caught completely off balance, and he flashed by Hayward five feet away. A great roar went up from the men as they saw Corado had been outmaneuvered.

In the same instant, Hayward was touching the horse's neck again. Still in its headlong run, the buckskin spun like a top. Corado had pulled his black to such a violent stop that it was back on its haunches. He tried to wheel the horse, but Hayward was racing right toward its rump. For an instant, it seemed that Corado would fall into the trap, his flank helplessly exposed as he wheeled into Hayward's thrust. But Corado must have heard the buckskin's hoofs thundering down on him. In the last instant he pulled his reins back viciously and reared his horse high.

Hayward could not stop in time. He raced directly beneath the black. He had to throw himself flat across the saddle horn to escape those flailing hoofs. He knew his back would be exposed to Corado as he came out on the other side. All he could do was veer the buckskin over. Its rump struck the black's belly, forcing the rearing horse to dance backward to keep its balance.

When the black came down, Corado was out of striking distance.

Hayward started to spin back. But he saw that he was in the same position Corado had been. Corado had now wheeled his horse and was racing after him. Hayward's turn would take him right into the man's thrust.

All he could do was put the spurs to his horse and race straight ahead. Corado was right on his tail. Hayward could not veer either way without exposing his flank to the man. Hayward was racing directly toward the rocky cliff. A great shouting went up from the crowd as they saw how Corado had him. Sooner or later he would have to turn, if he didn't want to smash head on into the rocks. But Hayward had seen Corado's deadly skill, and knew a turn now would be suicide.

As a last resort, he spurred his buckskin again. The horse dug in, gaining speed in a new burst, racing right toward the cliff. Another shout went up from the crowd, and Hayward knew he was gaining on the black.

Corado spurred his animal till his rowels dripped blood, but the horse could not close the gap. Then Hayward heard the sharp cry from Carlota.

"Juan!"

In the last instant, praying that he had put enough distance between him and the black, he turned the buckskin. It spun so close to the cliff that the stirrup chipped at the rocks. Hayward found himself face to face with Corado, who was charging down on him at a dead run. Hayward stopped the buckskin on a dime, with its rump almost against the cliff.

Corado saw that even if he struck Hayward, he could not stop his horse in time after the blow to keep from smashing into the cliff. He had to veer to one side or the other in that last instant, even though either direction would put him on the defensive again.

Hayward saw the frustration twist his face as he wheeled to the right. Hayward spurred the buckskin. It jumped like a jackrabbit. Its blinding speed closed the gap before Corado could turn again. And Hayward was riding Corado's rump, right in his blind spot.

Corado knew the deadly danger of trying to turn with Hayward so close. There would be a moment, as he veered, when he would be exposed to Hayward's thrust without being in any position to block it or defend himself.

The black churned the sand as it raced straight for the ocean. Hayward squinted against the stinging spray, sticking like a leach. Corado feinted to the left, and Hayward shifted to block him. Corado veered the other way for his real turn, but Hayward veered with him, blocking him off.

Corado drew blood from the black, trying desperately to pull away. But the buckskin was too fast, and he could not gain any ground. He feinted again, and again Hayward followed him and then shifted back to block the real turn. It was like cutting a steer from the herd. No matter which way Corado veered, no matter how many feints he made, the buckskin was always there, right on his tail, waiting for him to turn.

Then they met the surf. The salt water sprayed up from the flashing hoofs, and a foaming breaker broke into a million tiny pieces against the black's chest.

If Corado did not turn now, he would founder in deep water and lose all his speed, placing himself at Hayward's mercy. With a frustrated shout, he laid his reins against the black's neck, and the horse spun.

There was that moment when the man's flank was exposed, and he was in no position to block the thrust. Hayward was right on top of him, and struck.

But there was no shock of the blade meeting solid flesh. Hayward saw his knife pass through the air above the saddle where Corado should have been.

He had to catch himself to keep from pitching off with the impetus of his own blow. And his moment was gone. The racing horse, veering parallel with the shore as he struck, had carried Hayward twenty feet away from the black before he could recover and wheel.

He saw then what had happened.

Corado was just bouncing up into the saddle from the offside of the horse. As a last desperate measure, he had resorted to the old Indian trick of dropping off on one side just as Hayward struck, one foot in the stirrup, one hand clinging to the mane.

He wheeled the black to face Hayward, and then raced at him. Hayward knew he couldn't meet it standing still and kicked his own horse into a run. This was what Corado had tried to maneuver him into from the beginning. They were meeting head on, where the man's incredible skill would tell, where Hayward was not equipped to meet it.

Hayward knew he would have to rely on the buckskin then. It was his only chance.

As they raced toward each other through the shallow water, Hayward had a glimpse of the man's face. Sweat gleamed in the leathery seams about his mouth, his eyes were glittering with the insane excitement of the duel.

Then they met.

And in the last instant, as Corado lunged for his thrust, Hayward leaned back on the reins with all his weight. Cimarrón went back on his rump, stopping so violently Hayward was almost pitched off even though he was set for it. Corado's thrust went where Hayward would have been if he'd stayed in the dead run. But the knife whipped through the air three inches in front of Hayward, burying itself into his saddle horn.

Corado didn't have time to recover himself. Hayward had merely held his knife out, and the impetus of the other man's own running horse carried him right into it. The shock of the blow almost tore Hayward from the saddle.

The black raced on past, with Corado bent forward over the saddle, the knife to its hilt in his chest. Twenty feet behind Hayward, Corado finally rocked out of the saddle and fell to the sand, rolling to a stop at the edge of the water.

Hayward's buckskin was so excited he could hardly control it. He had to fight the lathered, dancing beast over to the fallen man. He stared down at Corado with no sense of triumph. There was only a deep sickness within him.

No sound came from the crowd of watching men. They sat their horses in silent awe, staring at this thing they had never conceived could happen. Hayward became aware that the firing had lessened in town. There were only a few sporadic shots. A file of blue-coated riders clattered out of the Calle Principal and galloped across the beach. It was Colonel Archuleta at the head of his dragoons.

The *fantasmas* on the beach made a belated move to rally, but the dragoons had surrounded them before they could move far, and Corado's death had taken all the fight from them. Hayward had guessed they would not hold together with him gone, but he had never dreamed his loss would shock them so deeply.

Archuleta rode over to him, seamed face smudged with gunpowder, one sleeve torn. He looked down at Corado, dipped his head at Hayward. "My compliments. We wouldn't have been able to defeat them if it hadn't been for you, Hayward. I think they really would have taken the town, if they'd been given till nightfall to gather, as Corado had planned. But not enough of them had come in, and they weren't ready." He chuckled ruefully. "They really did us a favor, without meaning to. Rodríguez tried to make a deal with them. He'd turn over the town, if they'd leave him in as *alcalde*. Every man in Monterey knows about it by now. If Rodríguez doesn't leave tonight, he'll be carried out on a rail."

He stopped, as another figure appeared on the beach, coming from town. It was Aline. She stumbled toward them at a half run. When she saw Corado, her face was blank with shock. Like a sleepwalker, she moved over to him, knelt beside him, took his head in her lap. The unutterable loss in her face made Hayward feel sick.

He turned his horse away. He felt beaten, unable to stay in the saddle any longer. He saw Carlota, coming across the beach, and rode to her and slid off onto the ground. She saw how drained he was and brought her scented softness against him.

"Don't blame yourself," she said. Her voice was husky with compassion. "It had to be done. I am more to blame than anyone. I was a spoiled child. I realize that now. I acted cruelly and thoughtlessly and took so much for granted."

"You were under a strain yourself," he said. "The responsibility of that whole big ranch dumped in your lap, the threat of the *fantasmas* hanging over your head. . . ."

"But if I hadn't treated Corado as I had, this would not have happened."

"It would have happened, anyway" he said. "Corado wanted you. That's what was behind his whole scheme. I think it had made him a little crazy, Carlota."

She buried her head against his chest. "I wish you weren't going now. I need somebody . . . I need you."

"I'm not going," he said. "I resigned my commission when I left that ship, Carlota."

She looked up at him, her eyes wide and shining. And he knew he had been right. A dozen other lands, and now only one. A hundred girls. And now only one.

About the Author

LES SAVAGE, JR. was born in Alhambra, California, and grew up in Los Angeles. His first published story was "Bullets and Bullwhips" accepted by the prestigious magazine, Street & Smith's *Western Story*. Almost ninety more magazine stories followed, all set on the American frontier, many of them published in Fiction House magazines such as *Frontier Stories* and *Lariat Story Magazine* where Savage became a superstar with his name on many covers. His first novel, TREASURE OF THE BRASADA, appeared from Simon & Schuster in 1947. Due to his preference for historical accuracy, Savage often ran into problems with book editors in the 1950s who were concerned about marriages between his protagonists and women of different races — a commonplace on the real frontier but not in much Western fiction in that decade. Savage died young, at thirty-five, from complications arising out of hereditary diabetes and elevated cholesterol. Such noteworthy titles as OUTLAW THICKETS (1951), THE TRAIL (1951), SILVER STREET WOMAN (1954), RETURN TO WARBOW (1956), and BEYOND WIND RIVER (1958) have become classics of Western fiction. However, as a result of the censorship imposed on many of his works, only now are they being fully restored by returning to the author's original manuscripts. Among other recent restorations of Savage's great Western stories are FIRE DANCE AT SPIDER ROCK (Five Star Westerns, 1995), COPPER BLUFFS (Circle V Westerns, 1996), MEDICINE WHEEL (Five Star Westerns, 1996), and COFFIN GAP (Five Star Westerns, 1997). Much as Stephen Crane before him, while he wrote the shadow of his imminent death grew longer and longer across his young life, and he knew that, if he was going to do it at all, he would have to do it quickly. He did it well, better than almost anyone who wrote Western and frontier fiction, ever. Now that his novels and stories are being restored to what he had intended them to be, his achievement irradiated by his powerful and profoundly sensitive imagination will be with us always, as he had wanted it to be, as he had so rushed against time and mortality that it might be.

THE BLOODY QUARTER will be his next **Five Star Western**.